Fighting Pretty

MISS VERA CAIN

British Athletic Girl

Gus Onlaw's
"Lady Boxers"

Fighting Pretty

Louise Walsh

seren

Seren is the book imprint of
Poetry Wales Press Ltd
57 Nolton Street, Bridgend, Wales, CF31 3AE
www.seren-books.com

ISBN: 978-1-85411-474-7

A CIP record for this title is available from the British Library.

Cover image: Getty Images: Sheer Photo, Inc

Inner design and typesetting by books@lloydrobson.com

Printed by Bell and Bain Ltd, Glasgow

The publisher works with the financial assistance of
the Welsh Books Council.

For Billy Summers and Ken Harrison,
Gary Thomas and Dai Gardiner
&
Mum

And in memory of
Pat and McCauley
&
Grampy

'And the loser now will be later to win
For the times they are a-changin'.'
Bob Dylan

CHAPTER ONE

These are the last of the men who remember the mines. They know all there is to know about digging deep.

"Here's where champions are made," says Dai Shepherd.

I look at the shed, the low mountain clouds bunched above it like a fist. Its walls, once the colour of ripe wheat, have been India ink-washed by rain, and dirt clings to the corrugated grooves in a green sludge thick enough to write your name in. A black roof sits on top, like a flat cap on a labourer's head. The front is punctured by a double metal door, at one time probably a cheerful cherry red, but now the lower quarter is covered in dark velvet moss.

Poster paper covers the inside of the windows but, where the corners have been torn, gold chinks invite a glimpse of the fighters shadowboxing, or a huddle of trainers talking and smoking. Even before you get that close, when you get out of the car and crunch across the gravel, you can hear the heartbeat of the gym: the thud thud, whump whump of the boxers on the bags.

Champions, that's what he'd said, *champions*.

Dai's words had been snatched away on the wind but they had been mine for a moment. I glanced at the 'old

Welsh legend', the northern gale ruffling his white hair. I'd half expected some opinion from him about women, or some comment about how times had changed. Back in Cardiff, women's boxing was something more than a controversial subject; they were two words that completely contradicted each other.

I knew better. I knew how hard women could fight when they had to, and Dai didn't seem to mind at all. They were more accepting in the valleys and I wondered why. Were they just tougher outside the city? These were old mining communities after all. They'd seen hard enough times when the pits closed. But perhaps they were simply more honest about things. After all, these days a gang of teenage girls can be as intimidating as any bunch of boys.

"Come with me," said Dai, as he swung the heavy door aside. He blew out through his lips. "Warm in here isn't it!" He tugged himself out of his coat. "You can change through there. We've got a changing room for girls, see." He moved me off towards it.

I hesitated as I pushed open the door. A Calor gas fire squatted in the middle of the floor and chugged out a fierce heat which rolled around the box room. I skirted a complete drum kit and a rusted filing cabinet and then backed into a large, eighties-style, dusky-pink scalloped chair and matching foot stool, which must have been provided by a wife or mother keen to make room for a new suite. The old-fashioned furniture was one of the room's more pleasant features.

The external wall and window behind the chair were streaked with mould. I looked up at the grey lace webs which clung to the ceiling and walls in tendrils. The smell of mildew was sharp and I shivered despite the heat.

I dropped my bag onto the chair, then pulled up short. By its side was a crumpled pair of navy Adidas tracksuit bottoms and, underneath, a pair of pink and white Puma trainers. Alana was here for sparring.

I stood in the doorway fumbling with my rope for a second, before joining two boxers skipping on a section of wooden floor. As I skipped, I spotted Alana. She was on a corner bag, a blur of hands: her back bent, weaving out of a roll. I turned my attention to the rest of the gym.

The trainers were dotted around the large blue Empress boxing ring, leaning on the ropes. They were watching two determined boys stalk each other back and forth. A wiry old coach, repositioning a black flat cap over a scalp of shaved strawberry blond stubble, cursed to himself. With a waggling finger he called one of the boys over from the ring. He put down a mug of milkless Tetley, took a quick drag on his roll-your-own and addressed the youngster in front of him.

"Babes... listen, Babes, look now... how many times have I told you? You've gotta throw that jab out. He's picking you off and you've gotta throw out that jab. You've had two rounds and he's picking you off and you're not doing anything about it, see. For Christsakes, Babes, throw the frickin' left."

Although he barked, he wasn't angry. His voice was caring and tired. He said it like he'd said it a million times to a million kids.

The hanging bags swung ripe as red chillies and crackled with hot flurries of punches, and a bunch of small children darted through the gym playing chase. The boxers were oblivious. A little girl, around four years old and dressed entirely in pink, stopped briefly in front of me and then ran off. Her laugh tinkled as she jumped onto a worn exercise bike a second before a little boy and pedalled furiously in delight.

"My granddaughter," said Dai, noting my smile. "Her father's American you know, so she'll be going over there soon. He tried to live over here but he couldn't cope with the weather. Too much rain and too bloody cold. I'll miss her when she goes."

"Let Dylan have a go now," he instructed her without glancing round.

The boy had run off to inspect the inner workings of the gas fire and so the girl, seeing her audience had ceased to be either captivated or irritated, clambered down from the bike. She headed for the strawberry blond trainer who was drinking his dark tea. The girl looked up, questioning him with her thick valleys accent.

"Tony, who's that by there?"

Tony stared back. "What's that babes? What did you say?" Tony dragged along his chair to make room for Dai as they both took a seat, and Dai sank down with a sigh.

She was high pitched and louder now, her accent more pronounced; Dai's little granddaughter strained to be heard above the rattling bags. She repeated her question.

"That's Lizzie," answered Dai, as Tony watched the boys in the ring. "She's come up by train all the way from Cardiff." Dai pulled the little girl to him and hooked a rosy button back into place.

She drew out a slow "oh" of reply, but her eyes were searching for Dylan.

Tony crossed to a dirty kettle, its plug lost in a cobweb gauze. It rumbled out a geyser of steam and he topped up the tea pot.

"So, you've been training with Cleto?" Tony asked me.

"Yeah, on Saturday mornings mostly... he's tough alright, he's... "

"You don't need to tell us what he is. George over there and Harry... we took him to the world title," he said with pride.

"George, come here a sec and tell Liz about Cleto. George trained him from a kid."

George looked like a generous grandfather; the sort who always has a story. The kind of grandfather that if you were to turn out his pockets you'd find them full of Werther's Originals, matchboxes with mysterious treasures, proper soft cotton hankies and a Swiss army knife. I liked him immediately.

"Cleto's been training you, huh?" he asked.

"You trained him with Dai, didn't you?"

There were posters all over the walls.

"Aye, so when you think about it, we've all contributed to your advancement. He's passing on our superior knowledge. Where is he? Did he bring you up?"

"No, Dai brought me. I didn't... "

"You didn't tell him?"

George looked amused.

"Cheating on him behind his back, eh?"

"Don't," I said. "I feel awful, but I need more sparring. I couldn't find anywhere else to learn. The boxing gyms – they wouldn't let me in."

"We let you in."

"Exactly, and the only reason I know about you is through Cleto. I don't know... I don't know how to tell him."

"He'll be fine," they assured me. "He'll understand."

I had tried bringing it up with Cleto, but I'd done it in such a round about way that he hadn't understood what I was saying. I felt guilty and it made me awkward. He'd been the first to take me into the ring. My last attempt to tell him I was thinking of changing gyms had been ambiguous to say the least. We'd just finished sparring and, as he took off his gloves, I struggled to explain.

"You know, Cleto, if you're up the Valleys gym on Sunday... any chance I could tag along? I mean... I'll meet you, you know, wherever, and pay towards petrol or something. I think maybe I should go up there sometimes? What do you think?"

"I would, but I'm not going this Sunday," he said.

I was running out of time. Cleto was about to go on holiday.

Tony and George looked amused.

"You have to pay, you know, if you're going to take advantage of our boxing brains," George instructed.

"I expected that. How much is it?"

"Well Babes, nothing at first until you come in regular. Then I'll start charging."

"How much?"

Their grins were catching.

"Go on."

"One pound per week, and George here is going to personally make sure you get your money's worth, aren't you George!"

"Personally," repeated George. "You'll get your money's worth up here. Now shut up and skip faster."

I glanced past the skipping boxers to the wall clock, hanging slightly askew with 12 o'clock not quite north. There were ten minutes to go. I flicked the rope quicker, relaxing into it as I warmed up. I enjoy skipping and it had been one of Cleto's favourite exercises on a Saturday morning. He danced inside the rope like Sugar Ray Robinson himself, and he passed as much as he could on to me. He taught me well. At one time Cleto had been asked by a former boxer to learn a *Duelling Banjos* skipping routine. It would have been fabulous, but Cleto wasn't convinced. However good Cleto was at skipping he wasn't the kind of man to play second fiddle, banjo or anything else.

When my time was up, I headed for a spare bag, noting where Alana was in the gym. I had only sparred with her once, and I knew enough to be aware that she had gone easy on me. It had been my first time in an exhibition, my first time in front of an audience, over at Fleur de Lys (Flower). It was over so fast I couldn't remember any more than three snapshot moments, but that was the night that Dai said he'd pick me up from the station if I wanted. Quietly, I pocketed his number and the strawberry blond guy had shaken my hand and said with a drawl that I had guts.

I did a few rounds on the bags and then they told me to get my gum shield. Alana got in the ring first, ducking through the ropes, no more than nine stone in weight. She had the frame of a footballer and short, cropped blonde hair. She greeted me with a serious "a'right" and the merest fraction of a nod. I smiled and caught a glimpse of myself in the mirrors; my big grin full of brilliant white gum shield. There were a few chuckles so I closed my mouth. The bags were still, as were the trainers. Everyone was watching. Even the eyes of the boys in the wall posters seemed to be twinkling with expectation: Cleto's girl meets the girl from Gelligaer.

"Time."

Alana and I touched gloves and the round began.

The ring felt different underfoot from the one in Cardiff. My legs were slow to get going. Whatever it was,

I was thinking of my feet when Alana landed the first rattle of sharp fists that set the tone for the whole three rounds. She was fast and accurate; her arms throwing out a drizzle of hard gloves. I felt exposed in front of the watching gym. My leads fell short and I was left plodding and thumping haymakers into spaces her shadow had long abandoned. I have heard boxing described as "theatre with blood". This was the Christmas pantomime.

"She's *behind* you!"

"Oh no she isn't!"

"She's behind you!"

Alana was Peter Pan in the ring that evening, impish and agile. I climbed out from the ropes after three rounds, eye smarting, embarrassed and grinning a wide lie of a smile.

"Sure, sure... no really, I'm fine."

In the main it was my pride that was bruised. I received my pat on the back and skulked off to the furthest side of the gym. I tucked myself away in the corner where I glowered at the Everlast bag under an imaginary dunce's cap. I aimed to improve, and improve everything.

For a few rounds the trainers let me alone. They stood talking among themselves, but then one broke away and ambled over. Even though the gym was warm he wore a cable-knit jumper over a stiff collar shirt and his grey hair held the ridges of recent combing. He took out the three tacks that had been pinched between his lips and placed them with a hammer on a nearby table. Then, after throwing a firm arm around the bag to stop it swinging, he clapped a hard hand on my shoulder, like he was greeting a friend he hadn't seen for forty years.

"I'm Ernie Ryan," he said, "and I train the amateurs with Tony. I was watching you in there. Stop throwing those hooks for starters, this is a boxing gym. We don't have street fighting in here. You understand? This is a *boxing gym* and there's no good just throwing all those hooks." Ernie demonstrated the punch I shouldn't be using, looping a slow arc in his M&S pullover.

"I want you to work on your jab, nothing else, understand? Start there, with the jab, ok?"

"Sure," I agreed, but I felt even more as if I was being disloyal to Cleto. What did he mean by street fighting? I must have picked up some technique from the Welsh-Italian world beater. Nevertheless, I couldn't deny that Alana had taken me into the ring and taught me a big lesson. It meant that if I wanted to stay in boxing, I had to get a lot more sparring.

Ernie smiled and rejoined the group.

When they thought I'd done enough they told me to stop bag work. My sodden t-shirt stuck to me as I pulled up a mat by the gas fire and started sit-ups. Steam had begun to roll off my clothes when I noticed a blonde woman sat on a bench by the mirrors, staring at me. It was obvious that she had come straight from work because she was wearing a buttercup-yellow nurse's coat with green piping and black trousers.

"You alright?" she mouthed, too far away to be heard. I nodded, inching away from the fire as she rose and headed over.

"I'm Alana's mother."

I said hello, introduced myself and complimented her daughter's boxing.

"She been boxing long?" I ventured.

"Oh ages," she said, smoothing the creases from the front of her tunic with work-worn hands. "She do love her boxing and football. She started when she was eight, wanted to try boxing so we took her down to the gym in Bargoed. She... well... she looked like a boy, so we didn't tell nobody, not even the trainer. We had to when he got her a bout with another boy though. The doctor would have told 'em anyway."

Peter Pan after all then, I thought.

"She got to sparring with all the boys then and let me tell you, she do go in there and cause them some bother. She probably likes her football more but she do run a bit funny, see. I think she's better at the boxing."

"Well, I can see why," I said.

I could hear Dai in the background.

"Christ, what's the time... I've got to get Lizzie to the station, ah, there you are... "

I grabbed my bags and coat, and said a rushed good-bye to the people I had met.

The journey back was quicker as there was a lot less traffic about. Dai asked when I would come up next, which days and which train I would be able to catch.

I said goodbye to Dai under a pewter sky. There were a few minutes before the Cardiff train. Once aboard, I touched the puffy corner of my right eye and dropped my head against the train window. Ignoring my reflection, I followed the line of hills as they turned the colour of slate.

As I stared at them I began to think back. For years my involvement in boxing had been no more than a weekly visit to Big Jim's boxercise. Mum put *the big change* down to the day Ian walked out, but it was convenient for her to think like that. It was simply a coincidence, perhaps, that on that day I had come in from boxercise; just before yet another domestic storm had left me grasping for an anchor.

CHAPTER TWO

That day I'd had my usual lazy-man's load. Why make three easy trips when you can have one God-awful humiliating struggle? I swore at myself in the hall of our Roath flat, battling with keys, shopping bags, gym bag, umbrella and coat. I could no more manage the rain-greased plastic handles and canvas straps than a sail in a rough sea. My feet edged round the door and flicked it closed on the freezing drizzle. Given my burden, I wasn't going to stand about apple-bobbing the light switch with a wet chin. I navigated a path to the kitchen mainly by good luck, carried on a foaming crest of white Tesco's plastic, and allowed the shopping to surf to a halt. Only half an hour till Ian came home.

The shepherd's pie was ready. I was confident he wasn't going to complain this time that it was too bland, or tasteless, or too *something* Ian couldn't quite put his take-out-ruined tongue on. I liked to make him food. It was February and I pitied him and the job he loved. Day after day he hunched over his mattock or spade in archaeological trenches; sharp brown eyes scavenging for Neolithic-worked flint or Roman coins, or any sign of humanity at all in the dark clay. His East German fatigues, a favourite with archaeologists, would be slack with heavy, glutinous muck. I pictured him at break time trying to be delicate with a skin of transparent cigarette paper. No matter how many times he wiped his hands on his combats, the water would seep out from his sleeves and get it wet. "A devil to light," he'd curse, rubbing a stubbled chin in frustration.

I knew that when his day was over, in whatever B & B he was holed up, he would soothe away his aches with a Chinese or Indian takeaway. He was happy in his way, eating hot and heavy food, his hairy legs lost under a thirteen tog quilt. I wanted to help him. I felt his tiredness.

It took me a whole ten minutes to unpick the broken oven door with the patience and finesse of a safe cracker. To shut it again took four hard slams until the lock caught – the temperature falling all the time. Finally I won. I'd have to speak to Frank the landlord, or better, get Ian to speak to him. I'd been asking them both for months.

It would take patience. We'd carried our laundry to the Soft Soap Laundrette for three and a half years before Ian could be coaxed into letting us get a washing machine. We always did things the hard way. I loved our new, quiet spin machine, so easy, so convenient and private.

The phone trilled in the living room. I loved that phone ringing even more than the new washing machine. Again, I didn't take the time to switch on the light, but sat in the grainy dusk cast by the kitchen bulb. Lazy-man's light. Kicking off my trainers, I tucked my legs up under me and hugged the handset.

"Hiya Boo, found the Temple of Doom yet?"

"Yeah, so amusing, and before you ask, no, I didn't find the Lost Ark either." There was a bitterness in his tone, which had got worse of late. I put it down to him being exhausted.

"Well, at the very least you've found the Temper of Doom so that's something. Just hurry up and get back because I've got a fabulous shepherd's pie you can excavate."

He was silent; refusing to play the cheer-up-Ian game. I teased him into action by reminding him he was on his mobile; such a waste of money if he wouldn't speak. Finances were his bug bear. Cinema trips had to be the early-bird bargain show. It had to be cheap or not at all: no coffee shops, no washing machine, only rented accommodation, clothes from Army & Navy, haircuts by yours truly. It was all the same. It was too expensive.

"Look... there's no easy way, I think it would be best if... if you live with your parents."

I would have done a fake yawn but the comment wound me straight up. I was still hot from the battle with the oven door and had no time for him banging on about the price of renting, *again*, as if he had been keeping me in the manner of a footballer's wife. Never mind five-star hotel holidays; Ian and I had a one star lifestyle – bed and board.

"Ian," I snapped. "Try putting your wife before your wallet. What about the emotional cost of me living with my father again? Thought about that, Sir Alan Sugar?"

"It's gone beyond saving money," he said. "I'm giving up the flat so you'll have to phone your parents. I'm... "

"...Completely insane?" I finished for him, with a fake laugh full of splinters. I hated these phone conversations with their awful anonymity. I wished I could stuff my feelings down the telephone and have his mobile explode like a small grenade.

"Ian, hummingbird, come on home. It's no good

talking about things like this over the phone." On the surface this was a white flag flying. In truth I wanted the battle closer to home with time to regroup. Let's fight this eye to eye, husband to wife.

"I should have said at Christmas... but I didn't know how to when you... "

Ian continued talking, but I stopped listening right there. We'd had a wonderful Christmas!

I wasn't being honest. The reason I'd made such an effort was that I could sense things weren't right. His manner had followed the weather, turning a chill north-easterly towards December. I'd worried that all the working away was taking a toll on his health.

On the weekends he barricaded himself in the spare room and played war games on his computer. It was more like a bunker. He smoked incessantly. Through the filtered light (for some reason he kept the curtains shut and a small lamp lit even in the day) I could hear the stuttering of machine-gun fire. He lived on cheese sandwiches and HobNobs.

It was a slow process at first, but Ian began to cover the wood-chip walls with war memorabilia. There were some British items but he had learnt everything there was to know about German collectibles. I said he was going too far but he had withdrawn too far to take any notice of me. Without saying a word, he turned our spare room into a military museum. He hung up scarlet flags emblazoned with black swastikas. Rows of bravery medals were polished and mounted. Cards and service papers were smoothed flat in plastic sleeves and displayed on cork boards. On a shelf above his computer German helmets grew like mushrooms in the dark air. In the corner a mannequin wore an SS uniform. I noticed enough to observe that sometimes he changed the tunics on the dummy. Other than that I stayed out.

Christmas was my cavalry charge. I spent hours making decorations. The drafts in our flat sent glitter and glue paper snowflakes spinning from nicotine-stained ceiling tiles. It was my antidote to his isolation. The festive spices of cinnamon, nutmeg, and clove did what they could to camouflage cigarette smoke and the smell of old army uniforms.

I made all the food myself, from the mince pies to the cranberry sauce. Big Jim had been an enormous help. He put together a menu and talked me through the preparation. He had trained as a chef and a marine before being a martial artist. As his wife Georgia often pointed out, he was "just like Steven Seagal in *Under Siege*".

The love and the food, together with the frivolous, hopeful gaiety of Christmas did pull him back to me, yet the fact that he'd still been thinking about leaving me was the first sign of my overall defeat. As the cliché goes, I had won the battle but lost the war.

"Still there?" Ian snapped me back to the conversation.

"No, I'm at Mum and Dad's house with a hankie on a stick!"

I needed time to think. This was serious. I rubbed my face with my hands, trying to gather myself... what could I do... or say, to make him change his mind?

"I'll phone Frank and give notice... the bond is yours," he continued. "I'll get a van next weekend for my gear. I figure you can chuck out anything else or sell it if you can: whatever."

My hands began to rattle with the effort of keeping control.

"Gee *thanks*, honey," I said through gritted teeth. "There's a great car boot sale over Splott. I'm pretty sure that's where the Hollywood A list go when they're fucking dumped out of the blue by their *bastard* piece of *crap* husband. Congratulations also, this is the first major decision you have ever made in our entire goddamn marriage, so *fine*. You live with it for the rest of your life, you *BASTARD!*"

I was still yelling my head off when, not surprisingly, he hung up. He was gone.

I called my mum, trying to explain what he'd said, feeling as weak and deflated as those old Christmas balloons. I didn't have the strength to talk above a whisper: sometimes dropping into minutes of confused silence. The anger came in a great surge. It wasn't only about Ian, because it swept up everything in its wake. It was a violent sea, marbled with white veins of spray, through which all past hurts were connected to each other. Feelings that hadn't healed, but had at least hardened, were again soluble.

Pointless tears came and I rubbed them away. There was silence at the other end of the phone, but I could feel my mum crying. I put the phone down.

The tide raced in.

I wanted a baseball bat so I could smash everything until it splintered. I wanted to bludgeon it all until my bat broke. The flat was a stepping stone... that's what Ian had promised when we'd moved in over three years ago. We had to put up with it for a little while until things got better. That's what I'd been telling myself. What was I to do now?

If I could have screamed without the neighbours coming round I would have. I could have shouted so loud the shockwaves would shatter the foundations. I wanted to carve up the kitchen; tear down the brick walls of the flat with my hands. I wanted to punch through the windows, rip up the carpets, bite and scram and blow up the whole fucking lot with a stick of dynamite. I wanted to stand in the debris of our marriage and cry.

I sank down on the floor and tried not to destroy what little I had left. I was alone in our cold flat on a Friday evening. The living room light was still off. The shepherd's pie hadn't finished cooking. Nothing had changed and everything was different.

I packed that weekend. If he changed his mind, I told myself, it was tough. Nevertheless, there were tearful breakdowns, fits of anger and a dizzy feeling of falling. I was watching my life from a distance. I was a spectator, shrunken and lost. I didn't have a clue how to get back. I saw my mum twice, her face pale and tear-stained. We pointed out things I would take and worked out how we would manage. I would have to dump most of it as they had little space. My lovely washing machine was the first thing sold. I didn't want to see anyone else at all. I particularly wanted to avoid both my dad and my younger sister. My sister was a textbook case in sibling jealously because, as the older child, I'd done everything first. She felt it left her with nothing and it was a resentment that had leached into adulthood.

"Oh, and there's something else," Mum added when she phoned later, "I'm afraid there's even less room. Your sister has decided to come home. She's decided she doesn't like her flat and... well... you know how funny she can get when you and I spend time together."

I was glad to return to work the following Monday, to some sense of normality. I'd been working as a secretary at Stephen Reynolds & Co Solicitors for a couple of years. Ian and I had been too badly paid for us both to continue working in archaeology and one of us had been forced to give it up. For the first time it seemed like I'd done the right thing. I had somewhere to go which didn't remind me of him. It was a tiny law firm in an ancient converted house. From the inside you had the impression it was being held up by the vast, dusty piles of Legal Aid client files. The anaemic building leaned against the modern red brick next door like a veteran on a grandson's arm. I knew how it felt.

I was embarrassed at having to explain the situation to my colleagues. One of the fee earners whistled "Ain't No Sunshine," on his way out. At least my boss, Lindsay, listened with sympathy as I explained how all I wanted was my maiden name back. Ian had left me with nothing, save his surname. I wanted to throw it back in his face. That afternoon, Lindsay came down and surprised me with a legal document changing my surname back to Collins.

"Lizzie Larsen," she said. "I always thought it made you sound too much like a cartoon character anyway!"

Having my own name back gave me a sense of being myself again. It reminded me that for most of my life I had lived without Ian and I could do it again.

I had to tell Stephen Reynolds, the senior partner, about the separation as I had booked Stephen's holiday cottage as a surprise for Ian's birthday. It was to be our first real holiday. He was a short man in his late fifties, with the beginnings of an award-winning comb-over. If it weren't for his Napoleonic presence he would have been lost behind his huge desk, which looked as old and creaky as the building around it. He frowned.

"Ah, I'm sorry to hear that," he said. "Did you have much of a history?"

"More like archaeology. Married three years, together for five, that's how it goes. Plod on, eh?" I didn't sound very convincing though.

"No worries about the cottage, but why not go alone, perhaps? Ideal opportunity? Contemplate your future in a large, five-bedroom luxury cottage only half an hour from the sea, with an acre of garden?"

"I don't think so, but thanks."

With a flat palm he ironed his hair smooth from left to right, thinking.

"Well, take a few days in any case. If you can't go then why not see if your parents want it? Do you have any friends? If you do, ask them. Oh, and before you run off, perhaps now is the time to tell you... now listen, I hate to kick you while you're down, but if I give Melanie's friend that job I promised you... well to cut a long story short, it saves me a helluva job buggering about with the bloody computers. Still, I suppose you've got so much on your plate you won't really mind, will you? And I am sorry to hear about Ian, he liked the Ramones didn't he? I remember you telling me that. A good group, yes, a very good group. I don't want to push my luck by asking for a cup of tea but if you're making one..."

Stepping over a stack of blue files I picked up the 'Best Boss in the World' mug.

I despaired.

Later, in boxercise, Big Jim bear-hugged me and almost caved my ribs in. He told me to call in and see Georgia after the class. When Jim came home, Georgia told him what my boss had said regarding the job I'd been promised.

Jim was forever the ex-marine.

"For starters you can stay here with us and secondly you'll give up that shit job on Monday or I'll kill you, or break your fingers or your legs, or do the lot."

I had to decline the offer of staying for all our sakes. Georgia, having attended a private school in Cirencester, was a model of English Rose reserve that I had no hope of living up to. I only cried at night or, if I really couldn't help it, in front of my mum.

Jim regrouped.

"Well, saying that, my sister India is staying next week so we won't have room for a bit anyway. Have you met her? Going out with a millionaire from London, you know. Perhaps it's for the best, but you'll give up that crap job of yours. Just think, take control. Get yourself some goddamn self respect. How good are you going to feel telling him to stick his job up his ass? Yeah, tell him to shove it, or I'll drop you off a cliff... for starters."

I ignored the voice in my head telling me that it was the wrong time to make life-changing decisions. I felt it might breathe a bit of warmth into me. I did want some control, and to feel like I had a say in what happened to me. The following Monday I handed in my notice.

Age twenty-nine, with no husband and no job, I moved back into my old bedroom.

"If you want a bit of pocket money... you could mow the lawn," my mum offered helpfully.

Oh crap, I thought.

CHAPTER THREE

My return home wasn't an ideal move. I had a difficult relationship with my dad. He was a man driven by anger, and my early childhood had been spent trying to keep out of the way of his explosive temper. He disliked children and was suspicious of women. He was darkly possessive of my timid and socially unassuming mother. He also suffered from mean depressions. There was only one time she stood up to him, and that was when she got a part-time bakery job to bolster his pay. He was furious at such an attempt at independence and remained so for the four years she kept the job. If I knew there was a chance that Mum would be home from work even a few minutes late, I would dawdle on the way back from school: a plain, shy loner with tombstone teeth and tumbleweed hair. Dreamily, I traced fingers around the soft cobbles of moss on the chipped, burnt-red school bricks, or floated autumn leaf boats along gutters till white water drains tipped imaginary adventurers overboard. There were a million other things better to look at than Dad's predatory pacing back and forth, ripping aside the curtains, his eyes narrowing with venom on the empty street.

"What time did she say she'd be home?"

Words snarled out. Dad was a man who said little without spitting it through gritted teeth, like chewing tobacco. An innocent question would be returned with a "What?" spat blackly to the carpet. As I grew into a teenager I would, with rebellious satisfaction, ask every question twice. Effectively, I shot the "What?" before it hit the floor.

"Do you want a cup of tea? Do you want a cup of tea?" I would politely ask.

Dad believed openly in the abject weakness of women and was fearful in a world where women could be your boss, cut you up on the motorway, divorce, and have fun without being married. We were a made-up, manipulative species and couldn't be trusted, in a truly innate, Garden of Eden, kind of a way.

By the time I was sixteen we squared up, wearing our principles like pistols. Who'll prove who wrong first? The whole family, shredded by discord, was tearful and begged me to live somewhere else. My boyfriend, Sixties Steve, who had a motorbike and no bloody respect, marked the end of family life for me. My parents were dumping my clothes in the driveway once a week and Sixties Steve was dumping me twice a week, as I often went on dates snuffling back tears and carrying a suitcase.

I lasted at home until a few months before my seventeenth birthday when I stuck up two fingers to my dad's house of 'whats' and my mum's acutely loyal loneliness. I ran off to Brighton.

Being back at home was uncomfortable. I still carried my legacy as outlaw and troublemaker so I made myself scarce. My absence annoyed them anyway, but I spent my evenings in the gym, at various fitness classes and in

the day I went to as many job interviews as I could.
I lost myself in Big Jim's boxercise class at Fitness First.
I loved to punch things. I discovered I had a natural
timing for it, which gave me a warm satisfaction. I wasn't
thinking of Ian as many believed: I forgot about him and
everything else while punching the bags.

The only other thing that made me feel better, if
only temporarily, was watching boxing matches that I'd
videoed. I watched a lot of fights, but I rarely taped
anything other than the featherweight contests. I liked
the feathers because they fought fast and hit hard, but
outside the ring they look like regular Joes. At the time
the Mexicans, like Barrera and Morales, were ruling the
featherweight division. The fight I watched all the time,
and still do for that matter, is the Marco Antonio Barrera
versus Naseem Hamed fight. It took place at the MGM
Grand in April 2001 and I must have watched Barrera
beat Hamed hundreds of times.

If you don't know the one I'm talking about, it wasn't
an out-and-out war like some boxing matches, Benn v
McClellan or Ward v Gatti for example, but it's a great
fight nonetheless. If you don't follow boxing, you've
probably heard of Prince Naseem Hamed anyway
because every little boy was doing impressions of him in
the late nineties. He's had trouble since he's quit boxing
and was rumoured to have been seen, weighing about
twelve stone, standing in a queue in McDonald's. It
doesn't sound much, but for a featherweight, the end of
the road is the drive-through of a fast-food outlet.

Back then, in 2001, Naseem Hamed was at the
height of his career. You had to admire him even if he
wasn't likeable. He was a dangerous guy in the ring, a
real psychological bully. He sneered at respected boxers

until they lost their temper, at which point Hamed took advantage of their loss of control and knocked them out. His punches were devastating. By the time Hamed fought Barrera he had won every one of his thirty-five fights, and thirty-one of these had been knockouts. A number of them were Welsh including Steve Robinson, Andrew Bloomer, Alan Ley, Miguel Matthews, Kevin Jenkins and Cleto Basiletti.

Barrera had a similarly impressive record, but without the circus tricks.

The fight started out the way most people thought it would. Naseem delayed the fight for forty-five minutes arguing about gloves; a thinly disguised attempt to annoy Barrera. After that there was all the tacky glitz: a backdrop of hissing fireworks, Hamed flying down to the ringside on a hoop, and an elaborate ring speech.

Barrera stood waiting. I won't go into every detail of the fight but let's just say they don't call Barrera 'The Baby Faced Assassin' for nothing. For all Hamed's psychological warfare, for all his clowning, the Mexican fighter was unshakeable. People began to wonder how long Hamed could keep the act up. Not long. By round ten the commentators observed that Hamed was "*staggering around like a Saturday night drunk*". Emanuel Steward, Hamed's trainer (who hadn't quite bought into the Hamed hype in the first place I thought) knew that short of a miracle Barrera was going to win and told Hamed to go for broke. Hamed's only recourse was to try to bully Barrera into making a mistake in the last round.

Barrera came out from his corner looking as fresh for the last round as he had in the first and calmly got to work. Then it happened. All Naseem's bragging and

leering contempt got too irritating for the Mexican. In
one swift move he stepped behind Hamed and marched
him straight into the ring post. After banging his head
against the post Barrera said something to Hamed. It's
said he whispered something like "Who's the daddy?"
The judges at ringside deducted a point from Barrera but
the Baby-Faced Assassin looked like he couldn't have
cared less.

The win was text book. Barrera had defended himself
at all times. I loved Barrera above all other fighters
after that fight, and I knew what I wanted. I wanted to
get life by the scruff of the neck and whisper, "Who's
the daddy?"

I found an answer watching Barrera.

It kind of woke me up. I wanted more than boxercise
classes. I had nothing, and therefore nothing to lose. I
made my goal realistic. I wanted to get my technique
right, and maybe have an actual fight. I resolved to do
everything I could to bring it about.

Eventually I landed a temporary job as a legal secretary
with Don Rankin & Marshall. My new boss, Michael
Harrington, thought of himself as dapper but only
reminded me of a fat ginger cat in a suit. Even being as
tall as he was, and he must have been six foot one at
least, weighing in at about sixteen stone, he walked softly
as a cat; padding up behind me on his hindquarters in
shiny, licked-clean looking shoes. He put his size down
to having constantly to entertain clients. He was big and
squashy with a warm Bagpuss smile and all the charm of
a spoilt housecat. The ladies adored him to the point
where he could voice things no one else dared. That is to
say, they allowed for the fact he had claws.

That's why I kept quiet in work about boxing. Michael had a hard enough time accepting the length of my hair. I'd had it cropped in post-relationship anger. Just washing that man right out of my hair, as the song goes, wasn't enough.

I was in his office when Michael's phone rang. He picked up the handset to be told one of his interviewees had arrived in reception.

"Excellent, what's she like? No don't tell me if she's in earshot, a number out of ten will do fine. Mmm, that high, huh? I'm on my way!"

No wonder I was having a hard time finding a job.

Later Michael arrived at my desk on his quiet paws.

"Listen Lizzie, I've just interviewed that girl."

"Oh, how did she do?" I wondered if she was higher than a seven. An eight and I would be out of a job.

"Well, now I think about it she had longer hair than you. Look, are you sure you wouldn't be happier with me calling you by a boy's name... more *comfortable* if you know what I mean?"

"Michael!" Our head secretary, Chloe, gave him a glower. "Leave the girl alone, she's not been here long. Anyway, how'd the interview go?"

"Not great, she plays women's rugby. What do you think, Liz? I mean *you* wouldn't play women's rugby and *you've* got short hair. Are you sure you're not a boy?"

"Look," I replied as sweetly as possible so I would be offered the job, "Billie Jean is not *my* lover if that's what you're getting at, and there isn't anything wrong with women's rugby."

"Ah, all a bit butch if you ask me, Collins. Well, so far the job's yours."

The job was mine. I found it a demanding although

friendly office and it was, at least, a job. Then there followed a second bit of magic.

Cleto Basiletti, a former opponent of Naseem Hamed, (therefore prophetically linked to Barrera) held a boxercise class at Llanishen Leisure Centre between eight and nine on Friday evenings. Because of the late hour I had never got there before. The centre was several miles away with a long uphill slog on the way home. But that night I noticed an acid-yellow Trek bike in the garage. It had been my sister's bike which she'd abandoned when she first left home. It weighed more than a Sherman tank and was about as easy to handle, but it would get me to the gym and back.

The following Friday I waited alongside the vending machines opposite reception, fidgeting like a kid before a Maths GCSE. The champ arrived and I held my breath. He wore a Nike baseball cap and kept his head down, concentrating on carrying a bag of boxing equipment that was bigger than him. I couldn't see his eyes.

Cleto wastes nothing and does everything with such an economy of movement it seems to defy science. He's tall for a featherweight, five foot seven and a half inches, and he carries more muscle in his legs than you'd think good for a feather, but you couldn't argue with his record. When he took off his jacket, his shoulders and biceps were smooth and hard as butterscotch. His dark Italian hair danced with every punch. The girls in the class adored him, and his innate passion for his sport. Those that turned up wearing full make up found themselves in a tricky situation. They wanted to look lovely for him but they frustrated Cleto because they wouldn't let themselves sweat. His job was to get them working and they wanted to wiggle and flutter at him. I wondered sometimes if this was part of the reason he seemed so guarded.

I stood out in that first class as I had done in other boxercise classes before. In Big Jim's class, the din of punching ricocheted off the walls of the lofty sports hall like hundreds of metal ball bearings being dropped on the gymnasium floor. Yet my punching was hard enough to echo above it all like pistol shots, only silenced by Big Jim's own efforts. I can't explain how or why I hit like that, but it worked best if I didn't think about it too much. My savagery on the pads meant that at times people would stop their own exercising to watch.

I couldn't explain it but I knew where it came from. It was a gift from my grandfather, on my father's side. In his youth he had been a fine boxer. It's said these things often skip a generation.

How I'd loved him. In my early teens I'd wound up visiting his grave quite by accident. After stealing yet another cigarette from my father's packet of Lambert and Butler, I'd wandered through the city streets. That time I wasn't running away, so much as getting lost. I wound up miles from home and realised I was outside the cemetery where he'd been buried. I got up the courage to ask in the enquiries office how to find the grave. They took his name and a rough date. I didn't have to wait long. They gave me a map and directions and I found the place easily enough. I smoked the cigarette on a bench by his grave. The place was silent, except for the empty swish of the breeze around the stones and rose bushes. There weren't many visitors. By the time I'd roused myself from my memories, the evening sky looked like a coal fire dying in the grate, choked with ash and burning embers. All of a sudden, I wanted to be home. The first time I punched something I understood that he had bequeathed me something special. And I felt his fire hadn't quite died.

Big Jim had taken my natural ability and tweaked it: telling me to hold my elbow a little higher on the hooks and to drive my right cross straight though the target. Soon people began to complain that I hit too hard; they didn't want to hold the pads for me. They were only there to lose some weight and get fit, not put up with someone as crazy about boxing as I was. Twice, when practising my right-hand-to the-stomach move on a person wearing a body shield, I brought them to their knees. Once I made someone sick.

I needed Cleto. You don't get to be world champ without knowing a thing or two about boxing. I had to learn to land my punches on a moving target in a ring. Without that, my big hits were wasted: something showy and useless, not to say annoying to my boxercise partners.

After his class was finished, Cleto called me to him. He looked me up and down for a moment and recommended I see him for personal training. It was obvious I had a natural talent for boxing, he said, albeit raw and un-trained. I took down his number, and with that he turned to pack up his kit.

I was so high on the ride home that I could have had ET in a basket, pedalling across the moon. So it took me a while to realise that I was making slow progress. Some joker had let my tyres down. I ground uphill as my pancake tyres turned the road to syrup.

The next morning I telephoned Cleto – *I was telephoning Cleto Basiletti, the Champ* – and made an appointment for Saturday morning. *This was it.* This was the start I had been looking for. He would teach me how to fight.

Cleto met me as I wrestled my bike off the train at Caerphilly. Though the station was only a short distance from the gym I was told to follow his car as he doubted I would find it without him.

I'd never been to Caerphilly before. I was mortified to be following the champ on my sister's bike and I wished I hadn't pulled at the masking tape on the handlebars. Like all these things it had been there for a reason, in this case to cover creeping rust. It refused to stick back, curling stiffly against my fingers. His personalised registration number read F1 GHT, as he glided before me in his sleek, racing-green BMW.

The Power Point Gym is an anonymous, grey warehouse, topped with a fat chorus of cawing seagulls. It caters for professional, executive types, including many consultants from Caerphilly Miners' Hospital. The car park looks like a prestige car showroom: full of gunmetal grey TVR monsters with red leather insides, and jet black Jaguars. My sister's Trek was, unsurprisingly, left untouched when a gang of magpie-like thieves pecked away at those shiny cars over a six-week period.

Right away Cleto said that he didn't think women should fight. I shrugged, because it didn't make any difference to me.

Five minutes later he wore an expression of surprise that remained frozen in place until I left. He knew I punched hard, but he hadn't expected me to charge with such vigour and aggression into every exercise he gave me. Big Jim used to tell me, "The trick is not just to run – but to run like you're being chased by a pack of wolves". That's what I did. I attacked the running machine and the press-ups; I attacked the sit-ups and the pull-ups and then, when we put on the guards and the gloves, I attacked Cleto as if my life depended on it.

At the end, when I had turned completely purple, he did say that perhaps women could fight and maybe he had been wrong. I only cared that I could go back the next week.

Big Jim had a favourite comment about my Saturday mornings: "If Cleto told you to cover yourself in feathers and stick a carrot up your bloody arse, you'd do it."

That wasn't true, or was it? No, not unless Cleto had said it would help me box better, then I admit there was a faint possibility.

After a few sessions in Cleto's classes I found myself stuck with a new training partner. On Edward's first visit, the woman standing next to me saw him, then edged behind me and ducked. He wore emerald shorts and a matching designer vest, from which sprouted undernourished arms and legs the colour of stilton, all white and blue veins. He bounded over and asked to be my partner. Why is it always me, I wondered?

Yet it turned out that Edward Creed was great. We were well matched in height, weight, work rate, endurance and pain threshold. The two of us became inseparable in the gym. I ignored his wardrobe and the fact that he gushed a steady stream of compliments that I soon realised meant nothing.

"Oh, that is great, brilliant, wonderful, fantastic, well done, superb... "

However tiring the continual and vacuous praise was, he meant well. I put it down to him being over eager to please and possibly some sort of Christian. He had a turn-the-other-cheek meekness.

When he asked me to team up for personal training, to split the cost of an extra training session on Wednesday nights, I thought it was a great idea. Off and on, Cleto would ask me to say something to Edward about his wardrobe. I refused. The more I learnt about Edward, the more I realised he'd had what they call a hard life. Things weren't easy for him. As a youngster, he'd been dragged around Nepal by a domineering army sergeant father. I saw in him the same unenviable mildness that my mum possessed. There was the same lonely, independent spirit which can stem from emotional hardship in childhood.

I grew protective of him, the way I felt about my mum. They both viewed their independence as strength, but it was simply reserve born of low self esteem. "Never ask anyone for anything!" That was my mother's most used phrase and it echoed through Edward. I thought it was a tough line: never to take but only to give, and keep giving, but it was how Mum had remained married for so long. She married a man who only ever took. Edward, never having had a proper girlfriend, had sunk into an apparently comfortable celibacy.

As an adult Edward had lost himself in London for a long time, working in helpful, subservient positions. He spent a number of years working in Claridge's Hotel. He returned to Cardiff out of duty, to become a carer to his widowed, housebound mother and her affectionate white poodle, Lily. The three of them lived in a dilapidated, damp terrace house in Gabalfa.

Edward wasn't sure about sparring at first, but he wanted to do the training and Cleto thought it would do him good to be able to defend himself. He thought Edward needed a bit of toughening up. I wondered how many times Edward had heard that throughout his life. He gave a brave smile as Cleto squashed and mashed a battered head guard over his thinning pate.

Cleto then stepped himself into the groin protector and wetted his gum shield. Cleto had learnt the hard way about sparring with non-boxers. They were dangerous because they were unpredictable. He'd once had four stitches to a cut after sparring with a newcomer who'd simply barged into him with his head.

Edward found it hard at first, and he also drove me crazy. If I punched him, he would thank me or tell me how great a punch it was. I thought it was some sort of strange, macho bravado and it made me uncomfortable. There were plenty of punch bags outside the ring which didn't wipe away a ribbon of blood from the nose and say thank you at the same time. My technique was raw and still I found him easy to hit. Lacking the basics, I trudged and stamped around after him, rearing up those right hands whenever he said anything complimentary. I thought he was making fun of me. The more he talked, the harder I punched him. Then I realised, with shame, that this was just his way.

"Oh, that is *totally* great, brilliant, wonderful, fantastic, well done, superb.... "

I went easier on him then, but Edward's style in the ring only grew more eccentric. Sweat splashed through his panted compliments: his arms seemed a fraction too short and he had a habit of bobbing and hopping from foot to foot. He was off balance and easily within range.

Before he knew it, Edward was sparring every time he turned up at the Power Point. The training with Cleto was intense. Each week I couldn't wait for my training sessions. I threw myself into it that summer and by the autumn I had undergone a complete change in shape; I was athletic and hardened. Edward's chest and shoulders had filled out. My desire to spar with other people grew. But I had never set foot in a real, amateur boxing gym.

The days became colder and darker. I tramped back and forth to work as car tyres hissed in the rain and brake lights bled onto the wet pavements.

Barrera was a million miles away.

CHAPTER FOUR

I tried to focus on the alarm clock, smacking the top of it until it stopped screeching. It was ten past five. My nose was still raw with the after-effects of a cold as I pulled on my favourite Puma hoodie and tugged my Adidas trousers over another pair of thick jogging bottoms. Cleto said the best way to lose weight was to wear two tracksuits while running and sweat it off that way. I paused at the window and studied the roof tops opposite. They were damp but the sky was clear. Staring hard I could make out a sharp prickle of stars. I knew from experience I would warm up as soon as I got going, despite it being December. Running was as routine as breakfast these days.

I ran down to the lake and it was beautiful even before the sun rose; the way the moon leaked mercury into the black water. Having circled it, I set off up the hill and breezed the steep gradient. I'd gone a short distance along the top road when my foot caught in the jaw of a broken slab and I was catapulted to the ground. I landed on my left elbow, which broke with a sharp crack under the pressure.

A passer by, however unlikely at that time of morning, might have thought I was lying on the pavement, not far from the big fir tree on Cyncoed Road. In actual fact I was underwater; washed over by strange currents of sea sickness. I was more jellyfish than person and it made a strange sort of sense that my broken bone, together with the rest of my skeleton, had apparently been washed some distance away. I was vaguely aware of a terrible pain but, while I knew it came from my arm, I was unable to place where that arm was in relation to the rest of me.

After drifting for some time, I managed to get to my feet and shuffled towards home like a deep sea diver, chains of lurid green algae drifting past in the chill morning. Sick and sleepy, I arrived home at last and tapped with my good arm on my parents' bedroom door. Mum answered straight away, her voice followed by a rustling of covers and squeak of floor boards. I listened. She hadn't sounded as annoyed as I'd feared. It sounded like she was getting dressed. I whispered through the door that I'd had an accident. I was exhausted and by the time Mum came looking for me I had made it to my room and sunk onto the bed.

Through my daze I was aware that she had reached out and touched my cheek. She whispered that she would wake my sister and left the room, full of concern. I was grateful. When I passed the mirror above the mantelpiece I understood why she hadn't questioned the seriousness of the injury. My face was grey with shock.

Contrary to the horror stories I had heard about people waiting for hours, there was just a solitary figure asleep on a bench at the Heath Hospital. The only other movement in the waiting room came from the hands of the hospital clock, which now read ten past six. A nurse led me to a cubicle for a blood sample. She missed her target and blood squirted onto the floor. A grey mist rolled in. I sucked in colossal breaths to steady myself and managed to whisper, "Excuse me. Can you tell me what blood type I am?"

Cleto was always telling me to find out what blood type I was. He had read somewhere that your blood type determined your level of aggression. 'O' type was a hunter and he said I was definitely an 'O'. He had never seen a girl who was more an 'O' than me. He had this idea that you could match your blood type to your diet and hey presto – you would be invincible. He told me to eat lots of red meat.

This was completely at odds with my father's mindset. He understood that women were gatherers. My genetics said that I should wear cotton dresses and pick posies of flowers. I should be dancing around a Maypole – not hitting people with it.

I didn't believe either of them, but I wanted Cleto to be right.

The nurse couldn't tell me what type I was, and it was all over the floor anyway.

After the X-rays, doctors flocked into the room. They settled in a V formation. The head doctor asked me when I had last eaten. I told him I hadn't touched a thing since the previous evening. In that case, he announced, they would operate straight away and their white coats fluttered as they migrated to the next patient.

I was processed with factory-line efficiency. I had barely finished filling out the forms when the morphine took hold. I felt great. It was all a big, happy adventure and everyone was so kind. I was curious about my new adventure... or at least I was for about five seconds.

I awoke in drugged confusion.

Had they done the operation? What happened?

With my arm lost beneath the thick crust of a plaster cast, I looked at the clock. It was 12.30pm. I dozed.

When I came round again, I had been joined by my knitted ITV monkey. He had been the sole stuffed survivor of marital collapse. His colleagues, Mr Potato Head and others, had been re-homed in the Cancer Research shop. I squashed up to Monkey with my good arm and accepted an offer of toast and tea from a nurse. Clumsily I tucked in, while the nurse asked how I had come to be there. I took a gulp of scalding tea, trying to rid myself of the dry toast cemented to the roof of my mouth.

"I was out running," I replied thickly, "and tripped."

"Running? Do you run up hills? Are you a hill runner?" She ruffled through a sheaf of yellow and pink papers.

I couldn't see the connection but I did run up Cefn Coed Hill and did do hill sprints on Penylan Hill. Another sip of tea and I could answer.

"Yeah, I do some running on hills. It's the easiest way to keep the weight off."

"Quickest way to destroy cartilage in your knees, ruin your hip joints and put you in a wheelchair by the time you're sixty," she came back. "You realise that? I used to do hill running so I know what I'm talking about. Mark my words," she warned as she headed for the door, "you'll be in a wheelchair!"

Just what I needed, I thought. The nurse had disturbed a number of depressing thoughts which I tried to choke down with the toast. I told myself it wouldn't make the slightest bit of difference. In a couple of days I planned to be back in the gym. A broken arm wouldn't stop someone like Barrera. So what if I'd never seen the inside of a boxing gym. *So what!*

They let me out the next day with a bag full of tablets that had me swimming again. I asked my mum to get rid of them. Glad to be home, I put the kettle on and I pulled out a mug for me and one for my dad. While the kettle boiled I went to change. I could smell the hospital on me; disinfectant and warm illness. I couldn't wait to get my running gear in the wash. Mum helped me manoeuvre out of my clothes. I wiggled my fingers through the torn elbow of my Puma hoodie, its front logo scuffed with dirt.

In the kitchen I waited, my dad was at the kettle, stirring away. He walked straight past me. With a shock of cold I realised he'd made tea for himself and left my empty mug on the counter, knowing its place. Of course, I thought, he wouldn't make tea for a girl. There were no exceptions. We make tea for men because it is our duty. I felt my type O blood coming to the boil.

Such a small gesture, but so huge to digest.

Right then, I was going back to work.

I tried to go back too. I got as far as the department Christmas meal where Nick, a solicitor, cut up my food. The next day my hand started to swell up when I tried to type. My cast clunked horribly on the desk, while all the secretaries went 'Oh, I felt that'. Utterly miserable, I was dispatched home again, but slipped round to Jim and Georgia's instead.

"Look at the state of you." Jim's arms rose like a builder's JCB, moving muscles like rubble. He rubbed the back of his shorn hair, regarding me with amused green eyes and something else – a touch of pious satisfaction? Was I being unfair?

"Yeah, great, right before Christmas," I sighed.

"You'll be out of training for a bit. Have you told Cleto?" Jim paused the K1 fight DVD he'd been watching. It looked like some guy was about to get his head squashed.

"Yes, he knows. I'm sure it won't be long though. You know me. It won't stop me for long."

"You'll easily be out for more than three months – easy."

"Oh, it's not so bad. The cast will be off next week. They don't keep it on so long now, gets in the way of recovery otherwise. Less muscle wastage if they take the cast off."

"You'll be out for longer than three months," he persisted. "You know, you may as well cancel Cleto for the time being; save yourself some money. I mean, work out how much you'd save if you're not training with Cleto for three months: it'll be a bit. You could do something else. Save for your own place or something."

"I can't cancel Cleto, you know that. Anyway, it won't be long, I can't punch with this hand but I'll be able to run and do other stuff, I've got three limbs still working fine." I wriggled the good ones for effect.

"You can't run like that, you crazy cow! The weight of that cast'll pull your back out! You can't punch. Face it, you've got three months off at the very least – and then I'll help you get back up to speed. It won't take long, not with muscle memory and your fitness."

"Sure, thanks, well... I'll keep it in mind. I best be off, you know, they'll be wondering where I am. Tell Georgia I popped by and I'm sorry I missed her."

"If I find you've been doing any training with Cleto I'll kill you myself," he said as he walked me to the door. "I swear to God I'll find you and kill you."

"I could fight you with one hand tied behind my back," I retorted.

I walked to Roath Park Lake, my touchstone, running route, hiding place. I drifted around the end with the islands; islands I'd dreamed of running away to when I was a kid. A thousand times I'd brought my troubles to a bench here. I slunk around to the opposite side, past the small lighthouse clock which matched my cast, plaster of Paris white. I took a seat. I'd been running around the lake in the dark for a while and it was good to see the park in the daytime. Autumn richness was long gone. A dry leaf turned and fluttered on the path like an injured bird. The naked trees caught cold sunlight in black nets of branches. I watched as their reflections in the water tried to trap the quick koi. A recent downpour had left the lake full, and pale gold stars winked in the small waves. My thin tears winked back. I sat alone on the bench until tiredness found me, and I trudged home up the hill.

Big Jim was right of course, but only about one thing. The weight of the cast was going to pull me out if I tried to run and if I was out of balance it would do more harm than good. Next morning I got up early and snuck out to the garage. I dug through the deep drawers of terracotta garden pots and garden string until I found my sister's Velcro hand weights. One was enough, wrapped around the good arm. I crept carefully down to the lake and orbited as usual. It worked, there was balance.

I had been out of hospital three days when, at 8am on December 13, I wrestled myself into my gym gear and started out for the Power Point Gym. With my inability to ride the Trek it was a long journey. I ignored the weather warning.

If it hadn't been so stupid then it might have been funny. As I reached Caerphilly, the aching, petulant storm clouds let go. I was blinded by a splintered mirror of hail and sleet. A savage wind sent a thousand shards of ice spinning through the air. My wet cheeks were scratched scarlet, my fingers useless. The wind drove at me, trying to throw me backwards. I struggled to keep my plastered arm dry. By the time I reached the road to the gym, hot tears were dripping off my chin. I sniffed and wiped at them in case the champ rolled by in his car. I knew I was behaving like a lunatic. I should have stayed in bed but I couldn't stop myself.

I did the training with the cast on, punching with my right hand, doing sit-ups and squats. I was as careful as I could be, but when it hurt like hell I yelped and the plump seagulls outside in the rain swooped and laughed.

Cleto's wife, Susan, had given him an early Christmas present. It was a camera phone he had been after and he was desperate to try it out. He flipped the lid and insisted that he take my photograph. I thought of the photo used in evidence against me. I saw Big Jim, one hand on the witness box in the courtroom and the other holding up Exhibit A, glaring at me.

"Is this, or is this not, a digital photograph of you, training with Cleto Basiletti at the Power Point Gym, three days after your operation – with your cast still on?"

"Um...it's me."

"And were you not instructed that I would kill you if you went?"

"Um, yes, yes... you did."

"I rest my case, your Honour."

Cleto took Exhibit A as a smile struggled out from my pinched face. My hair was damp and still windblown. My shoulders sagged with shyness and the uncomfortable cast. "There you go," he offered. I looked at the screen. It is an understatement to say that the picture was monstrous.

When the car park magpies snatched the new phone from his car a few weeks later I selfishly hoped that he'd deleted the picture. I thought again of Exhibit A and Jim's judgment.

"Does the defendant have anything to say?"

"Yes, m'lud, I could fight him with one hand tied behind my back, m'lud."

CHAPTER FIVE

I spent a great deal of time at Roath Park, my escape from the Christmas family rows and pervading loneliness. I sat on my hands, keeping them warm as I admired the lake; grass banks covered in a milky frost while the sun rusted the last brittle leaves on the trees.

I loitered, thinking of nothing and everything. I watched the visitors as they strolled off their Christmas puddings and brandy butter, escaping the smells of stuffing and cold roasts. They made me feel hopeful and lonely all at the same time. Their steamy breath rose as they walked, a slow queue of coats, collars stuffed with tight twists of bright scarf. Across the lake they became funny, bulbous bundles, thick with woollens, shoulders squared against the wind. I wondered how their Christmases were going.

I missed Ian and the way I'd rest my head on his tummy watching films while he smoothed my hair.

I grew quieter as I recovered from the injury. In private, a painful and rigorous physiotherapy was going on. Every day I worked my elbow and arm, rallying its stubborn stiffness through exercises given to me by the doctors. As the aching joint became more mobile I bought a small rubber ball, which I caught time and again with my damaged arm as it clicked off the pebble dashing at the back of my parents' house. The commitment and obsession I once put into learning to box, I now focussed entirely on healing myself.

I learnt about tea tree oil, a 'natural antiseptic', and lavender oil, for healing scar tissue. These were mixed in carrier creams applied religiously four times a day until my skin was saturated. I took cod liver oil and glucosamine sulphate supplements 'for joint care'.

The pain tore up and down my arm, stabbing down to my wrist and back up. At times it played games with me. The agony would subside for a few days. Unconsciously, my shoulders would relax and I'd feel lighter. Then, the next day, I would wake to find the pain had trebled overnight. Did I jar it in my sleep? I wondered how long this could go on as I swallowed more Ibuprofen.

Twice the pain was so awful that I panicked. I wanted to go back to the hospital. I thought the pins had moved and I cried with horror, thinking that they were working their way out from under my skin, the way a splinter would. You saw it on the news; the body can reject lots of things.

Then Dad said something that stayed with me for a long time after. It's something I'll never understand. I have heard worse things, but perhaps it was my own unhappiness, with his words ladled so cruelly on top, which made his outburst more terrible.

"I'm bloody glad it hurts you! You know that? Bloody glad it *hurts!*"

I thought of asking why, but knew I didn't want to hear it.

I wanted to kill myself.

With Dad, Ian, boxing, my broken arm, the daily grind of work and never having any money, I couldn't see the point of anything. I couldn't imagine it getting better. It was a mystery to me. People were a mystery. Things never seemed to change. I couldn't remember the time when I had last smiled and meant it, but I knew it had been a long time ago.

Suicide would, of course, only have been a cry for help. I couldn't cross the bridge on the way home without wanting to hurl myself over the railings and there was a morbid element of fantasising about it. I was haunted with mental images of my own death.

What saved me, if anything, was the knowledge that the bridge was most likely too low. I might survive. I might have to spend my days as a suicide survivor in my parents' house. It would *really* never get better then. Life would be confined to sitting next to my dad in a wheelchair, craning forward for a plastic straw as he turned up the volume on *Bergerac*, *Lovejoy* or *International Bowls* to drown out the sound of my still being alive.

That's why I boxed – right there. I hoped that punching would lengthen my arms enough for me to reach right round to my back and pull out the knives.

I hated Ian so much it hurt. I hated him for sending me back to people who so despised me. I hated him especially because he wasn't there to crush me against his chest or brush the tears from my wet hair until I went back to sleep. I wouldn't have minded if he'd have come back in the night only to dump me in the morning. *Fine by me, Boo, just snuggle.*

It was late July before anything started to change. Cleto realised that I needed a little more experience, so he drove me up to have a small exhibition at the Fleur de Lys gym, one round boxing with Alana, and another with a girl called Jenny. It was there that I met Dai and Tony who told me about their history with Cleto. They said that they had lots of people for me to spar with. Dai offered to meet me off the train if I ever wanted to visit.

Weeks rolled by as I agonised over how to tell Cleto. We got on well and I didn't want him to think there was anything wrong with his training. It was all I could think about as he gave me a lift to Caerphilly station on a Wednesday night.

Cleto was talking about Oscar De La Hoya. He'd seen every one of his fights. After a thoughtful pause, when the hard rain chattered between wiper swathes, Cleto couldn't keep the excitement out of his voice.

"You know, De La Hoya is fighting in Vegas in September. He's fighting Bernard Hopkins. I'm thinking of making a holiday of it."

"That sounds great," I nodded.

"Yeah, Las Vegas!" he continued. "There's nothing like seeing a fight in Vegas. I'll use a gym over there too, get a bit of training in. I wish you could come, but maybe next time, maybe we'll make a thing of it for all my clients. Imagine – if we time it right you could get to see Barrera fight. How good would that be?"

Joking, he punched me in the arm.

I stared out into the night as sleet fizzed off the orange streetlamps like water droplets spitting off soldering irons. I felt terrible. Already knowing he was going away, I had called Dai the day before to make arrangements. He wouldn't know I'd changed gyms until he got back.

As Cleto was most probably out on a morning run through the pre-dawn cool of the Nevada Desert, I was in work at Don Rankin & Marshall Solicitors, listening to Jill Bridges. Jill was excited and told anyone who would listen that she was accompanying me on the train to meet Dai Shepherd at Ystrad Mynach station. She enjoyed playing mother, even though she already had two children and eight grandchildren.

It was hard to pin down Jill's exact age as everything she wore was straight out of New Look or Topshop. She had been one of the first to wear the slouch boot to the office and the first with the season's must-have tasselled poncho. The fact that she had crocheted a poncho for her granddaughter while watching Coronation Street, might have been a clue to her date of birth. She couldn't knit due to occasional bouts of rheumatism but the poncho was well within her crochet capabilities and she sold them to anyone who wanted one. I put in an order for two. They were fine but I was unable to wear them. Their handmade woolliness took me back to school days; knitted jumpers and knotted hair. Mum's needles clicking through the summer, driving my dad to distraction, and ticking away the minutes until the autumn term. I was the kid with the same style shoes as Sister Mary Peter or Sister Mary Andrew and it always seemed to take one of my classmates only half an hour to notice. The first week was always punctuated with the same sneer.

"Did your mum knit that for you?"

That was kind of how it felt that day at the office. I could almost see those knitting needles, like clock hands tangled in a nest of old wool. The count down was over and I was hopeful, but preoccupied with convincing myself I didn't care how the first day went.

"If I don't keep an eye on you, you'll be getting off at Pontlottyn and Dai'll be doing his nut," Jill chided.

The other secretaries smiled. Some of them welcomed the diversion and made the most of the opportunity to rest, chin in hand, for a second. Don's is a busy office and, being a Wednesday, it was far enough into the week for the girls to start looking for a quick break in the afternoon. I also relished Jill's lively warmth and was grateful for the unexpected maternal fussing. I didn't have much confidence in my ability to travel alone; I was too distracted by trying to keep out of a mental school yard.

The girls in the office still had a glint of amusement about them when, at five to five, Jill and I logged off our PCs and with a hasty "see you tomorrow", we got out of the building and hurried over to Central Station. Jill had explained the trains to me the day before.

"If you go to the nearest station to Don's then you have to stand all the bloody way to Hengoed, so we'll run further over to Central and get seats."

As she was, I can only guess, just a few years off retiring, and wearing red, beaded flip flops, the nearest thing Jill could do to running was give a commentary on how her feet were killing her but, as she had promised, we got there in time. Breathless and relieved we slipped through the station entrance, Jill's flip flops echoing off the cool stone floor. The station was packed and Jill and I worked our way through the commuters. We sped up then, up the staircase to platform six, picked out for us by a little brown hand laid into the old yellow tiles.

As Jill twisted through the train to get a seat, we bumped into a conveyancing fee earner from Don's. I hadn't spoken to her before but knew her by sight, as her white-blonde bob was hard to miss in the office. Fay and Jill were, I quickly realised, very old friends. They settled straight into banter about their weekend, filled with too many double vodkas and mysterious "flying chicken". This later turned out to be chicken and chips from Caroline Street, hurled into the air by Jill when she took a drunken fall. Jill introduced me, fluffing up her feathers proudly like a mother hen.

"I'm taking her on the train to see Dai Shepherd. Did you know he was in school with my Colin? Well, she's going up to his gym tonight and she'll fall asleep and end up in Rhymney or something if I don't take care of her."

I smiled sheepishly at Fay as Jill leaned forward in her seat and I knew what was coming.

"Come on Lizzie, tell Fay what time you're up running in the morning," Jill said, nudging me gently. "Fay, it's not even light! What time did you say, Liz? Five o'clock? She's out running, and in the rain too, at five o'clock in the morning... and I thought I got up early!"

"Dear Nelly!" Fay exclaimed. "You're out on your own? I hope you have a mobile phone on you," she clucked.

Jill edged in a little further with feigned secrecy towards Fay, trying to build up the suspense in the carriage, while her voice got a little louder so as not to leave anyone out.

"So anyway, she'll only forget to get off or something and Dai is meeting her off the train because she's going *boxing*!"

It had the desired effect. Three people in the carriage glanced at me furtively, expecting Tyson-style facial tattoos, chipped teeth or at the very least a broken nose. I presumed they were disappointed. I looked like any other office worker on the train that day.

Jill asked Fay when Daniel was home next and I learnt

that Daniel was Fay's new partner. Fay told me that she had been widowed three years earlier, days before Christmas. It was something Fay wanted me to know straight away and I could feel her urgent need to show her emotional scars so I wouldn't judge her without knowing. She told me so I wouldn't be thinking that she'd had it easy; wouldn't be thinking she was too lucky. She took a sharp intake of breath.

"Right then. He worked as a butcher in Tesco you see, and just before Christmas Henry went off to work, like normal. Anyway, one of the girls from Tesco's, she noticed that the light was off in the butcher's so she went to have a look. When she switched on the light there he was on the floor. He was still warm. They said the paramedics worked on him for ages but they couldn't bring him back, you know. He'd had a heart attack right there, hardening of the arteries they said."

"Jesus Christ!" I sympathised.

"Yeah, right before Christmas."

Fay raced through the narrative so quickly and breathlessly that I wondered if we would be getting off the train soon, thinking perhaps she was worried about having the time to finish telling me of her loss.

"Thing was like, he wasn't supposed to be working that day but they had these turkeys coming in for Christmas... no, wait... I *thought* they had turkeys but they never did. Anyway, he wasn't supposed to work that day in any case, but really thank God because I couldn't have coped if he'd have passed at home. What would I have done? Just imagine! Or what if he'd died next to me in his sleep? Christ... I don't know how... I don't know... it would have been too much. You know what," Fay ran on without stopping. "I can't go into my lounge now for any length of time, 'cos that's where me and Henry used to spend our time. I sold all my living room furniture, all good heavy wood, let it go for nothing and I'd had a dining room table delivered the week before and everything. I had to get all glass, totally opposite, you know, completely change the room. Well, I mean, when I say I don't go in there, I mean I clean and go in when someone's visiting of course. Sometimes I'll watch TV in there if I know Daniel is on his way but otherwise I still kind of stay in the bedroom or watch it in the kitchen. I'm gonna have to move one day aren't I? The sooner Daniel is down here the better. I don't *do* living room."

"Sure," I nodded.

"I don't *do* living room," Fay repeated with emphasis. "Can't, flat out, *can't!*"

"Sure," I said quietly, reassuring.

"There's too many memories. I used to clean everything too, obsessive see. I'm still bad but not like I was. Always cleaning the kitchen floor. Maybe I would go in the lounge more if Daniel was home all the time but he works away a lot with ASDA and I feel... "

"Right... "

" ...feel a little bit like Henry is sort of still there. I'm never going to get used to it but then I met Daniel, totally unexpected, totally a chance encounter. He's from Leeds and he'd do anything for me Jill, wouldn't he? I mean, he was different too and that was a really good thing. I couldn't have gone out with someone... too... I mean he... "

"He sure is... " nodded Jill with a chuckle.

" ...well, that he... you know, he wasn't really anything like Henry, even total opposites to look at. I know I'm very lucky with Daniel 'cos he's really very nice. He's, you know, he's..."

"Wonderful," Jill offered.

I smiled sympathetically at Fay and she shrugged and smiled back. She had shared it and now we were friends, I didn't think she was too damn lucky at all.

Jill and Fay got back down to their weekend recap and I thought about Fay and her husband having a heart attack.

I was distracted eventually by the hills and valleys we snaked through in the evening sunshine. Plump, nude clouds blushed in the low sun like fat little cherubs against a pastel blue sky.

Some of the mountains you pass up there look ancient, brownish-grey with a scattering of bristly, scrubby trees on top. They remind me of the backs of sleeping elephants. You can imagine an old zoo keeper giving them a wash down with a stiff brush and a bucket of soapy water. Others look like they're fashioned from jade, with carved clusters of winter-green fir trees and lush, grassy fields. Seeing them for the first time I wanted to run their entire length until they turned the soles of my running shoes green. I lost the thread of general train conversation in the beauty of those hills, and it was a good thing after all that I had someone there to tell me when to get off.

At Ystrad I grabbed my bag and thanked Jill and Fay who stayed on until the next stop. I stepped off the train and walked straight past Dai waiting there on the platform in front of me. Hearing a furious tapping coming from the train I knew it was for me. Jill and Fay's laughing faces were pressed up against the window while pointing wildly at Dai Shepherd. I grasped my mistake and knew all the secretaries would hear about it the next day. They were still laughing as the train pulled away and I saw them relax back in their seats, their motherliness justified in the knowledge that they had helped me out.

I turned back towards Dai and smiled, thinking that he must have realised what I'd done with all that rapping on the glass, but he hadn't noticed a thing.

"Thanks Dai," I said as he pointed out his car.

"Anytime you want to come, give me a ring. Is that the only train you can get from work? Any earlier trains? I'm just thinking of the traffic see. I was stuck down the bottom of the road for ages... "

I listened to Dai talk in enraptured silence, so happy to be there. He smiled and his blue eyes crinkled as I put my seat belt on.

" ...take no notice of the ABBA, it's my daughter's tape. D'you know we had the female pro fighter, Rachel Cleaver, in the gym a few years ago? Sure we did, she asked Cleto for sparring, or was it Gazz? Anyway, I think it was Cleto and he said no. It was different then... they sort of... well, they didn't like sparring girls but she was down a few times.

"I was hoping Cleto would take over the gym, especially as I'm not well. When I was diagnosed I told all the boys to find somewhere else. It was going to be too much, but they're all coming back now. I had twenty-five pro fighters at one stage, yeah, twenty-five, maybe more when I was over at Flower. I was training and managing Tommy Duggan. Now *there* was a *fighter*! Such a waste... such a bloody *waste*!"

Dai looked across me to get a better view of the road as he signalled. His eyes were unexpectedly bright. Sometimes you can tell when people aren't well because their eyes give them away first. You could believe from Dai's semi-transparent skin that he was unwell, but not from his eyes. They twinkled at me for a second before he looked again in his rear view mirror and turned. There was enough light flashing in his eyes to remind me of Gower rock pools, sunlight fracturing the cold water. There were enough points of dancing ice-blue to tell of fight and life and humour just beneath the surface.

"When I started," he continued, "I was the youngest manager in Wales and now, get this – I think I may be the oldest. I've asked Cleto a few times if he'll help, but he's so busy training people in Caerphilly. Still, you know... I might ask him again sometime. He's in Vegas I hear.

"It's a different world now in terms of training. I've seen them down the Vale when I go for treatment, charging a fortune and using those enormous fitness balls."

As Dai drove through the steep streets, he pointed out areas of interest and where various people lived, though I'd never heard of any of them.

"Right there is where the pit used to be, Yvonne. Of course, it's been closed for ages."

Dai talked with such relaxed conviction that for a moment I might have believed that my name was Yvonne. I strained to see over the hedge, and wondered who Yvonne really was. Was she of one of his daughters? He had four daughters altogether and, if what Jill said was true, they weren't girls to be messed with.

Dai took a sharp right and headed down a lane hidden behind some houses. There followed a further hard left into a car park and he slowed to stop in front of the big butternut shed, from which came the sound of leather being butted by gloves.

My heart skipped a beat with joy.

CHAPTER SIX

The trainers at the gym had worked down the mines and they all wanted to know which solicitors I worked for. Many of them, or their brothers or cousins, had proceedings percolating with Cardiff solicitors who represented them for vibration white finger or silicosis from coal dust inhalation. Looking around the gym, it seemed almost too bright to be connected to the mines. Dust dazzled like fool's gold in a shaft of copper sunlight, slanting off the mirrors and burnishing Brazil-nut-stained floorboards. In this natural spotlight four boxers rose and fell, performing double-under moves like springs inside their speed-ropes. American flag punch bags swung like wrecking balls, the steady thwacks sending their white stars shooting. I looked up towards the ring where the pro, shadowboxing alone inside the ropes, spat a white gum-like gob onto the canvas and rubbed it in with his peacock-blue boot.

Ernie caught my eye as he turned up *It's Raining Men* by The Weathergirls to drown out the sound of the clattering speedball. Both Ernie and Tony had spent their working lives in the mines. The men in the gym were descendants of bare-knuckle fighters who had rolled up their sleeves on the mountainside as well as in the claustrophobic coal caves, black as space. I imagined Tony and Ern's lamplight illuminating galaxies of soot particles in noise as thunderous as a NASA rocket launch. Tony told me of the time when three and a half tonnes of machinery fell on him and he showed me a two-inch-wide scar, which twisted round his thigh from his knee. The miners' spirit was still in the gym; in the sweat-greased men, chipping blindly away at the bags and grinding out their moves to the last.

"Dig deep, Lizzie," they called "dig deep."

There was nothing they couldn't tell you about digging deep.

There was also the fact that the raw stench which roared around the men's toilet door would have killed a canary.

By the autumn I was having regular lifts off Dai. I got the train to Hengoed instead of Ystrad because the traffic was lighter, and waited on the station wall as small yellow and orange leaves rolled down the chilly street like marbles. Being sat on that wall, with nothing to do other than watch for Dai's car, would start me thinking. There was nowhere else in the world I wanted to be other than the gym and I was well aware just how strange and unconventional this must have seemed to others.

Dai picked me up Tuesdays and Thursdays and reserved the front seat for me while the back seat became a sticky fudge of children. They loitered, like me, on various corners for Dai to sweep by and scoop them up. Skinny white elbows and scabby knees jostled for position. "The real back street boys," Dai would say, nodding at his rear view mirror.

"I see Dai's been around Hengoed with a net again," Ernie often said.

I loved being there. I loved being caught in Dai's net.

The gym walls and ceiling were a patchwork of pictures, photos and discoloured clippings from newspapers and old boxing programmes. As I skipped I read the stained, ivory-coloured tatters: full of stories. What were all these boys doing now? There were lists of names everywhere and it made my skin prickle with sadness that we were all just passing through the gym. Why couldn't I stay forever? The lists clung on thanks to a dusty wisp of tape or a lick of long-dried glue. All these valleys boys who'd chased a fleeting dream of winning in the ring and then moved on.

Ernie and Tone walked me around the walls one day, filling in the background on some of the names and faces pasted there.

"See, that's Andrew John," Tony said. "Andrew's brother boxed here too about ten years ago. They buried Andrew last year. Overdose, aye. And there's Sammy. Eh, remember Sammy, Ernie?"

"Who? Let's 'ave a look. Ah, little Sammy, Sammy the Sandwich Kid 'cos he looked like he never had a proper meal in his life. He went off the bridge five years ago. Never seen a fighter with such heart as Sammy. He'd never back down that one."

"It's got to be six years now."

"Never! Six years? Let me see... aye, you're right. He was a lovely kid, quiet like. I went to his funeral. He had his problems, see. Boxing... it do keep 'em out of trouble for a bit but sometimes I think their hearts are too big. Too big for life an' its cruelty sometimes, see."

Ernie filled me in on fragments of gym history while he

fixed things or vacuumed. The gym, he said, was split between the pro and amateur trainers. George, Harry and Dai had the pros on Tuesdays and Thursdays. They were legends, those three trainers, and in the 1980s seconded the likes of Frank Bruno, Lennox Lewis and Barry McGuigan when they boxed in Cardiff. On Monday, Wednesday and Friday he and Tony looked after the amateurs. The gym had been bought in Hull, dismantled there in five sections and reassembled on the Welsh hilltop. The gym door, Ernie shouted over the squealing vacuum cleaner, was from a prison in Plymouth and weighed a ton.

Ernie said if it was food or drink I was after then George was the man, although Tony did a good line in trout if the season was right. It seemed that every story they told me about people drinking George's blackberry wine ended with them passing out, then someone finding them and thinking they were dead. From time to time, George brought in giant vegetables that he grew in a greenhouse, including an onion he cultivated which was almost as big as a basketball, its skin like parcel paper.

"It can't taste like a regular one," I said.

"Exactly the same," he promised.

I didn't know they understood. I thought my troubles were hidden by boxing. They weren't blind though. I had washed up at their Plymouth prison door holding in so much hurt I couldn't recognise it for what it was. I was in a twisted sort of pain: the sort where a hug can make you cry like you've just been born; where a little kindness can make you cry worse than if you've chopped up a Godzilla onion. Some of us, it seemed, were sporty, and some of us were sad.

Alana was sporty, and boxing was just one of the many

sports at which she excelled. She was a natural boxer. I tried to learn from her and worked so hard you would have thought I was earning money for it.

"How many rounds you done, Lizzie?" George asked me the same thing every night as he clicked his red stopwatch. I always lied about the number of rounds I did and everyone knew it. I wouldn't stop training until they made me stop, clocking up around fifteen or sixteen rounds, sometimes two minutes, sometimes three minutes a round. After a while, they got George to watch me and try to stop me at eight rounds. When they asked me how many rounds I had done I would say seven. Two or three times a night George would ask me and I'd give the same reply: seven. Even little Dylan seemed to know it was a lie and would give me a shy smile and then jam his face into George's jumper.

In the end George would make it clear that it was time to cool down with a couple of rounds dodging imaginary punches, my feet planted on either wall of a car tyre (cue hilarious jokes about spare tyres). After that it was floor work, a cup of tea and home.

George became curious about how much I really did in the gym. He began counting out my numerous seven rounds with pennies on the side of the ring. As they lined up he would shake his head saying, "she'll get her money's worth!"

Back and forth I raced, like my left jab. I ran three to five miles before going to work, did seven and a half hours typing, then caught the train and met Dai, sparred and worked out in the gym, caught the train back and then boarded the number fifty-seven or fifty-eight bus for home. It didn't take me too long to realise I was going to have to learn to drive.

I did it in four months. Edward volunteered to teach me as he had once fancied becoming a driving instructor. In addition I had a mad French teacher, with floppy hair like Gerard Depardieu, who gave me one lesson a week shouting: "You should 'ave turned herlier!"

Edward's car was a pitted, dirty blue-grey Volvo, spattered with the crusty crappings of birds and city dust. I was grateful that he trusted me with the car. I lurched it around an industrial estate on empty Sunday mornings and it clunked and cut out, leaked oil and gurgled greedily with the attention. I practised hard, delighted that he was so patient with me and ignoring his relentless "oh, that is *TOTALLY* great, brilliant, wonderful, fantastic, well done, superb... " comments, while I clipped curbs, stalled, and tried to slap off the wagging windscreen wipers. To thank him, I gave his car a good clean but to be honest, the thing only looked more faded and pitiful, like those donkeys you see abroad. I wanted to start a collection to send it to a Volvo sanctuary.

I asked my boss about buying a car. It seemed simple when he explained it. You get a loan for what you can afford and then you go shopping for the kind of car you'd like to drive within your means.

It was this sort of ignorant independence that almost finished my father off. Someone like me going to the back of beyond and buying a car while knowing nothing about these things. Who the hell did I think I was? Just who the hell...? He was not a big fan of women drivers.

You should have seen the car though. I'll probably be sat in an old folk's home one day, hunched and dribbling over my jaundiced corn-beef feet and mumbling about the day I bought that car.

The Mini was parked sideways on, the sunshine bouncing off it in rays, and its metallic red drowning out every other car in the forecourt. I was so dazzled I didn't really see any of the other cars at all. I didn't even try to bluff knowing anything about Minis or car buying in general. It was *my* car and it was waiting for *me* to collect it. That was my walnut dashboard and those were my cream leather seats. When they delivered it, I soaped and waxed it to a sweet, liquid finish, like cranberry sauce. I christened it by tying miniature, scarlet-leather boxing gloves to the rear view mirror. It was the first grown-up thing I'd owned. And it was the happiest day.

"I'm so pleased you've bought Baby," the garage owner said.

It was the most perfect car in the world.

I took out a small loan to pay for Baby and found I had enough left over for a bond on a flat. I had the great idea of putting an ad in the local paper saying I needed to rent a flat and naming some of the areas I remembered Dai driving through on the way to the gym. When a lady called saying she had a flat in Pontllanfraith (not on my list) I got it mixed up with Penpedairheol (on my list) and by the time I realised, it was too late. Looking out of that bedroom window I was sold instantly on the most amazing view. Once in, I positioned my bed so that when I woke I could watch the ponderous rain clouds as they crawled down the valley on battleship-grey bellies, or the white squadrons of clouds, like silent ghost Spitfires, turning their wings towards Cardiff in the breeze. I never closed the curtains. Since childhood my family wondered why I slept with the curtains open but I couldn't understand why you'd sleep with them closed.

You didn't need curtains when it was dark because, well... it was dark. At dawn surely everyone wanted to be up moments before a mere thumbnail of sun rose and flicked out a shower of gold and pearl across the vast midnight blue?

The guys at the gym asked me why I moved to a place four miles away. I shrugged. I knew they'd say it was the sort of stupid mistake someone from the city would make. The flat turned out to be only a few streets away from where George lived, and after finding that out, I was quite content.

I was a valleys girl then, and it meant the end of training in Caerphilly. I was relieved to stop sparring with Edward. On Wednesdays, he had begun to ask about going to the Gelligaer gym. Cleto refused to allow it. He said that it was best for Edward to stick to the training side of it, that there was a chance he could get hurt. They'd been training together long enough for a real friendship to develop between them but, with his hopes dashed, Edward grew noticeably colder and thoughtful.

I had to agree with Cleto. Edward's style hadn't changed much. He hopped from heel to heel and jerked his head like one of the pigeons who crapped all over his car. He had a mean punch, when it landed, but the truth of the matter was, he was just too nice. Edward finally steeled himself to come up to Gelligaer, after weeks of wrestling with his conscience as I had done, but neither of us realised Cleto would be visiting that day. Cleto appraised his Power Point runaway from the other side of the ring.

Dai Shepherd was looking in better health than he'd done in weeks. He had a pink glow about him as I introduced him to Edward. Dai smiled, and told him to spar with me first because he was used to that. I hugged one arm around a bag and waited for the boys already sparring to finish their round. Cleto meandered over and gave a quick nod.

"A'right Liz?"

"Sure Cleto," I said. He wasn't one for small talk. I expected him to say something about Edward.

"You sparring with Edward next? Well... go easy on him. As easy as you can."

"Okay," I said. He walked back to the other side of the ring.

At first I was flattered. I wondered if he was implying that I would outclass Edward. However, as soon as the sparring started I realised something was wrong. I cut down Edward's movement until he was in the corner and then threw a couple of hooks to his ribs, nothing too hard. He tried defending himself but his hands were strangely slow. He tried, with a minimum of effort, to get out from the corner. I couldn't believe he'd get in the ring if he had no fight in him. I pecked my left jab at him to test him, trying to encourage him out of his shell. He had been the one who'd kept on about coming up to the gym but I'd never seen anyone start sparring looking so defeated.

Edward must have noticed my frustration growing because he put up his guard to protect himself. I planted my feet. They were all still watching. I looked at Cleto, hoping for a clue as to what I should do, but he wasn't looking at me.

I grabbed Edward in a headlock and jokingly rubbed his head guard with my glove. The trainers in the gym understood I'd stopped the sparring for some reason and they called time.

I didn't understand Edward at all. The other trainers didn't know what to make of it either.

"Is he alright, that Edward?" Tony asked.

"Yeah, I think so. Oh... I dunno."

"Tell him he can come up here anytime he wants."

"I have... we'll see."

"How's the car? Ernie wants to know if you're going to need a jump start again. He's missing it. What's it been now, two clear nights?"

"Don't tempt fate," I said. "Baby's running fine now, just perfect. It's the weather up here that's doing it. I thought everyone was joking about the difference in weather up here. It's not this cold in Cardiff."

"You'll find it's two overcoats colder than this in Bargoed and five colder in Tredegar. Now, while we're at it, George saw you on the hill a couple of nights ago, when he was taking little Dylan over his friends. Aye, he was behind you in the queue of traffic and he said you were riding the clutch. You'll wear out the frickin' clutch like that. Use the handbrake."

"I know, he's already told me off. It's a habit I got into."

"Get out of the fricking habit!"

"I will, Tone."

"And get yourself a frickin' hat while you're at it. You'll catch your death, and while I remember, I've got something for you."

He wiped his mouth on the back of each hand in turn and searched his pockets. Finally, he held up a new silver key. I had to make a solemn oath to lock myself in if I was there alone and not open the door to anyone. I wasn't to tell anyone I had it and, if I promised all these things, then I could use the gym whenever I wanted. I could call it a second home; I felt like a sort of fighting Snow White.

I counted my achievements now on the loop of a key ring. And at last I was approaching my first fight. My first two bouts were only a week apart and both against Alana. It goes without saying I lost them both. Life is not a Rocky film. In real life the person who is better wins and if you have to fight the same person a week later then the person who is better wins again, just the same.

Alana had always had the upper hand in sparring so I was pleased with my efforts and thankful that I had only a few supporters there to see me lose my first fight at Blackwood Rugby Club. Edward was there, as was Cleto.

No one came to the second fight, which was some way off, but I was sure that wasn't why Edward didn't turn up. It wasn't like him and I wondered whether I had done something to upset him. Cleto said Edward was obviously depressed, having realised his secret hope of marrying me wasn't going to work out. Somehow I doubted it. By December it was clear that he had, at least for the time being, left his friends in boxing. I accepted that the friendship had run its course but I missed Edward with his infuriating optimism. I could only assume he had his reasons and, more selfishly, I was too preoccupied with my fight to ask for an explanation.

CHAPTER SEVEN

Christmas came again, with the same tired, circular routine. Before lunch was served I was thrown out by my dad. As I was about to drive away I was begged to stay by my mum. I stayed for her but I vowed it was the last time. I'd lost my appetite for tradition.

I was beyond miserable. A couple of hours later I was back home and tearfully ramming down a whole box of chocolates. If I had to explain, I'd say I ate them like I hated myself. I ate them like I didn't care anymore; like saying to myself I hope you choke. I ate them in the exact same way you'd feed someone you couldn't stand. I came face to face with how terrible I felt about myself and it's not easy to shock when your only audience is yourself. You'd think there would be few surprises. I needed to turn back the clock and not only because I'd done such a spiteful and immature thing, but also because I was supposed to be watching my weight. In those few minutes I had eaten more calories and fat than I'd normally get through in a week.

I knew I was going to make myself sick. I also thought I could eat something else before I did it. I thought about the food I could try, food I had denied myself for

months, even years. I spent Christmas night head
down in the bathroom wearing a toilet seat halo. I felt
disgusting and I felt better at the same time. I told myself
that I was in control again, but deep down, as I ran a
bath, I knew control was the last thing I could call this
spectacular mess.

New Year's Eve was spent hiding from the world in the
Tredegar Junction with George. He didn't ask how my
Christmas was going. All he said was "I'll be a father to
you". I hugged him and he smelt warm; he smelt of beer
and Brylcreem. He was a calm, family man. I imagined
him on Christmas morning rolling out more pastry for
the mince pies and calling out cracker jokes to his family, while little Dylan tried to take the living room door off
its hinges with his new tool kit.

It wasn't an easy decision to visit the Junction. It would
confirm I had no one else to spend New Year's Eve with.
Still, I didn't regret going; sat alongside George with his
shrewd and squiffy smile. He introduced me to everyone
there, and then, as the evening went on and the drinks
kept coming, he forgot and introduced me to everyone all
over again.

In January there was something to celebrate, Presentation
Night arrived at the Gelligaer gym. The activity was
frenetic as tables were upturned and lathered, chairs
wiped and mirrors rinsed. I watched as the layers of dust
and sweat ran down under Dai's sponge in a fringe of
muddy rivulets. Green apple air freshener clouded the
ceiling and corners. The ring and woolly grey carpet
were vacuumed, the floor swept and a disco assembled
outside the ladies' changing rooms.

The transformation was startling. The hanging bags vanished and were replaced with a buffet put together by Tony's wife. There were quartered pasties, sausage rolls and triangular sandwiches stuffed with cheese and onion or skinny slices of ham. The lights were turned out and bright swathes of disco neon chased each other around the room. The thirty-six chairs were soon full and guests sat on the ring sides and steps. They sang along to the music, clinking their bottles and hunting for ash trays.

I leant across the table trying to hear one of the sponsor's wives. I could never remember her name, but she worked in the same office as Edward. Her husband was a huge boxing fan, having followed Cleto's career from the start, and he often sponsored the amateur fighters. They were always at boxing shows. She tried to shout a question to me over the music for a second time and I cupped an ear in her direction.

"Sorry," I said, "I didn't catch that! Who?"

"Edward, have you heard from Edward?"

"No, it's funny, I haven't seen him for a while and I don't think a day went by last year when I didn't at least have a text from him. How's he doing?"

"I think it was the knockout that did it, don't you?" She touched her husband's sleeve to get his attention. "The knockout, didn't we say we thought it might be that?"

He nodded without looking. "Possibly."

She had my complete attention now. "What knockout?"

"It's all round the office. He wanted to learn to box, didn't he. Cleto told him he'd come on as far as he could, but there was no point him taking it so seriously at his age. He wanted him to stick with the bag work. So Edward got the number of this guy who said he could train him. On their first training session together, the 'trainer' knocked him out. It happened about a month ago, just before we went skiing. He was awfully embarrassed in work. You can imagine. The bosses had a talk to him about it. Terrible black eye! Perhaps you could give him a call; check he's alright. I mean, it's not very *nice* being knocked out, is it, not when you think about it... not *really?*"

Why hadn't he told me?

The following day I waited in the payphone box that doubled as the betting shop ashtray, growing frustrated with the dring-dring of Edward's inert phone and the fact that I hadn't topped up my mobile. Then he picked up. He sounded relieved that I'd discovered what had happened. As he began to fill me in, I searched my pockets for more coins, anticipating a long stand.

"You see Liz," he began, "I had a load of problems already. Something needed to be done at home with my mum. It was getting on top of me. I needed help, didn't know whether I was doing too much or too little. I didn't know who to speak to... to set things up, what organisations might help, and the worry kept coming back. When my mind wasn't on that, then there was always something in work I was worried about. Kind of like when you are doing too much and not giving yourself a moment to take a break or rest and suddenly everything just drains out of you, everything suddenly comes to an end and you want to throw in the towel – with everything, Mum, training... see Liz, my life seemed to have had the bottom taken out of it and there was nothing. So my mind wasn't on that morning.

"Anyway, this trainer-person boxed me in the corner, excuse the pun, and my arms were wide open. He was huge, an English ex-pro, and he works as a bouncer. He saw the opening, like he would in a normal fight, and maybe he knew I might catch him and do a little bit of hurt. I suppose he was acting on instinct but I didn't see the upper cut at all. I was too square on and literally like an open book, he even said that after, he said "you were too square on". He caught me smack in the centre of my right eye. Well, I dropped where I stood and couldn't see or think but was clean knocked out. To be honest I didn't know what had happened...

"Eventually I came round. I rolled over onto my back and tried to open my eyes. My sight in my right eye was completely black and the left blurred, and I was confused because it all happened so fast and I sensed that everyone was looking at me. There was this other guy who had been doing an exercise on one of the machines and I knew he was walking towards the ring. Sounds pretty bizarre, Liz, I know, that I knew he was coming over when I couldn't see at all but it was the silence. I heard him, or rather, couldn't hear him training anymore.

"The trainer leant over me and he looked dead worried. He got down on his hands and knees, put his arms around my back and lifted me up. He asked me if I could stand and I said 'yeah, I'm fine but I have a bit of a problem with my right eye. I can't see anything'. He said we would get out of the ring and have some water.

"The other man came over to investigate and he was horrified. He said, 'Oh my God that's already coming up!' Then my trainer patted me on the back and said to me, 'Come on, let's do some light weights'.

"We carried on training. It took me about fifteen minutes to get my bearings back and then I was really worried because this terrible pounding started in the back of my head which came and went, on and off, and for the rest of the session I couldn't focus. It felt like someone had rammed a poker in my eye, burning, and I wanted to rush to the mirrors and pour water on it and see what had happened.

"I ran to the mirrors in the changing room and I saw it was not my usual black eye – much more serious and you know what I thought? I thought: 'you shouldn't be going through this at this time of life'. I mean, I'm forty-five Liz, and I work in an office! It was already puffed up and underneath looked lined and old and my eye was completely bloodshot. Plus all round my cheek bone there were these lines and swelling, red lines, like someone had put red paint on my cheek. Not the sort of redness when you've been out in the cold but much deeper. Then after about a couple of hours the focus started to come back but then the pain seemed to move away from my eye to my cheek and jaw bone.

"See, the way he caught me, vertical, you know, the angle of my body was all down and it was his instinct and discipline to deliver that punch in that type of way and I was standing just perfect for it."

Then he started explaining how embarrassed he'd been by the reactions of his work colleagues. I butted in.

"Edward, tell me you've been to the hospital."

"Well, I wasn't going to but then these nose bleeds started... "

"Jesus, tell me you've been, I'm not kidding... you have been haven't you? You have seen someone?"

"Not really, Liz... I didn't know whether... "

"You have to go right away! If you don't go then I'm going to take you myself. Please Edward, please go to the hospital."

I begged him until he backtracked and promised to call me in work the next day once he had gone. That morning

I snatched up the phone on the first ring of every call. He rang in the end.

"I did it. I went for a scan at the Heath Hospital Liz, and, ok, I'll say I'm glad I went because the doctor said some really nasty bruising was showing up behind my eye and it looked as though there was still blood there. They said there was bad damage to the tissue behind the eye but, thank God, it hadn't affected the retina. You know what he said though? He said, 'If you continue, you'll lose the sight completely'. And the consultant said it was possibly the fact I'm so fit, which means my blood is very thin, that had saved me from getting a blood clot which could have killed me. Liz – I was going to get in the ring for more sparring with him!"

"You aren't serious?"

My tone was sharp enough to surprise the office boy who had ducked his head round the door looking for someone. I put up a hand in apology and nodded.

"Yeah, last Wednesday he called me up and said we'd do some light sparring again if the muscle in his back was feeling better. He'd pulled a muscle doing weights you see!"

"Aw, poor thing," I said.

I asked him why on earth he had gone training with someone like that, but he had no real answer. I pointed out that he had Cleto, and didn't need to be proving anything with seasoned ex-boxers who didn't know the first thing about him, and who didn't care either. I made him promise to keep in touch.

Edward walked away from it all though. He stopped training altogether and decided to take up running. I next saw him in March when he came to Blackwood Rugby Club to watch me fight again.

"I wouldn't miss it for the world," he'd said, with that eagerness I never got used to. "Who are you fighting?"

"D'you know, I'm not sure. Tony hasn't said much about her... I think she's from Newport."

"That's strange. So you don't know what she's like or anything? Is that good or bad?"

I hadn't thought about it.

"I don't know, Edward. Anyway, how's the head?"

"Still hurts, Liz... and... well, sounds funny but when I look in the mirror I can see this shadow..."

I could see it too and, moreover, I still had my own.

CHAPTER EIGHT

As Edward found, months after a walloping hard punch to the face, long after the bruise has gone, a shadow can remain. I received my mark many months before from Big Jim, in an impromptu sparring session before boxercise. I turned up early for one of his classes and he wanted to see what progress I was making with Cleto. What started out as a bit of a fun fight quickly became competitive and it was as much my fault as his. He landed a right hand with such force that I wondered how he hadn't broken my nose. Our fight continued, without rounds or referee, until the rest of the class turned up. When the bruise faded it left a greyish band along the bridge of my nose, which I believed might be there for good.

My third fight did nothing to help it on its way.

I was lost in the melee of the chilly changing rooms at Blackwood Rugby Club. Groups of skinny lads hopped and danced, pulled on socks, did up laces, and tried to keep warm. Trainers jostled in and out. "Sparky – go and see the doctor, Ricky-lad, you're on first round." They compared boxing boots, whispered about other boys and threw sideway glances of respect at the current British

Champion, who'd popped in to lend support. He was wearing his trademark cream beanie and leant against a table packed with paper plates of food. One of the boys lifted the cling-film on a plate, his loosely bandaged hand like that of a Halloween mummy, and helped himself to a handful of Quavers.

Alana sat looking tired as she coughed through her shoulders. I wondered whether the doctor would let Alana box at all. It was that time between seasons and I had a slight cold myself, though not so bad it would have any effect.

To free up space, Alana and I were sent to the main function room where the boxing was to take place. We stood with our backs to the radiator, inside the door, shivering in our shorts. Neither of us said much; simply stared at the empty ring, which seemed to be getting smaller as the room filled up. My mouth was dry and we exchanged a brief word about not having seen our opponents yet. We acknowledged that we were both nervous and that the room was packed. I shrank back against the hot knuckles of the radiator as a group of men slopped past with pints and cigarettes. Alana coughed again.

As she waved a hand at the thinning threads of smoke, a girl strolled past, chin high, wearing a smart tracksuit, her hair woven into a French plait. "That's her," said Alana. "That's Vicky, the one you're fighting. I don't know where mine is."

I couldn't swallow. I knew little about Vicky other than that she had been, like Alana, fighting for years and had the sort of reputation in boxing that necessitated facial expressions rather than words. When I explained I was fighting Vicky, people puffed out cheeks, rolled their eyes, or whistled a 'phew' sound through their teeth. For a time I thought it yet another conspiratorial wind up, but after a week of watching people's faces contort, I stopped asking.

"Hiya Lizzie, we found it at last!"

I turned to see about ten of the secretaries from work arrive – at the same time as my ability to speak went right out of the door.

"So when are you boxing? Have you seen who you're fighting? How many are... "

"Hiya Lizzie, it took ages to find but we stopped and asked at the... "

"Oh, Liz, I can't wait... it's the first boxing match I've ever... "

"Is that the ring? It's bigger than I thought... so are you feeling nervous or... "

"Is it true that Michael said you're sacked if you get a black eye or... "

"I'll be back now," I said, "...have to get some water... see you guys in a minute."

As I headed back to the changing rooms I passed another self-possessed girl, looking so wiry she might have been twisted by a sculptor. Her eyes were full of hard confidence and her face was thin, almost gaunt. I guessed it was Josie, the girl who'd be fighting Alana.

I was glad to escape the questions, the shouting from the bar and the smell of alcohol and cigarettes. I made my way back to Tony, who was busy scribbling out the fighters who had failed to turn up or make the right weight. As I entered the room he looked up and told me I was on after Alana so I may as well go back in and watch. The youngest boys were on first.

I returned reluctantly to my colleagues and frowned in

concentration as two young boys came out. The first lad was Ricky, who boxed out of our gym. He'd had a bleached Mohican in celebration of his first fight and marched with a soldier's serious pride, swinging his gloves, left, right, left, right, all the way up to the ring.

"Oh, aren't they cute," came the cries from the secretaries. "I want to take them home!"

By the time the third round ended their folded arms predicted what was coming.

"Oh, they're so little, surely it's not right," one of them said.

Ruby stood with one hand on her shoulder bag and the other on a hip. She looked at the boys collecting their trophies and then back to me.

"Someone wants to call the NSPCC, that's what they want to do. They're *children*, making them get in the ring to fight each other! It's not on, really, in this bloody day and age!"

"Wait," I said. "You see Ricky, the kid with the Mohican, he wanted to fight me in the gym the other day, honest. He couldn't wait to get in there, Rube... and the other kid, the kid who lost, he thinks he's Muhammad Ali. You wouldn't worry if you could see them in the changing rooms... they're indestructible and they're too light to get hurt!"

"I don't care. I don't like it. They're only kids. I can't stand stuff like that... I am... I'm going to call the NSPCC!"

"Honest, Rube, no one forces them to get in there. It's just a game and it keeps them fit. Anyway, the kids are done now and Alana's on next."

I missed most of Alana's tough exhibition with Josie, answering question after question about children and boxing and how often the shows were put on. As they entered the last round I dashed off to be helped into the gloves.

Tony squashed down the tight blue head guard, like squeezing a lemon, and the room was suddenly much quieter. I didn't want the colour blue. I wanted it to be red. There was no reason for the preference, it had materialised out of nowhere, a surprise of superstition.

Tony took hold of my face in his hands, my cheeks pillowed in the hateful head guard. I haven't met one fighter who is comfortable about wearing them. I didn't even know where they were kept in our gym. Tony looked me in the eye and I was deaf and blinkered to all but Tony and his instruction that I wasn't to let her intimidate me, I was to fight hard.

"Time to go."

I smiled at Alana as I followed Tony down the corridor. As she passed me I heard her complaining to her friend, "Tony said I did crap... I don't know what was wrong with me... "

I wondered what Tony would say to me if I was terrible.

Vicky got in the ring and bounced on the balls of her feet. She looked the part. Her clothes matched – and she had fringes on her shorts, the kind I had only ever seen professional fighters wear on TV. I wore stuff Tony had found for me. Ernie shoved in my gum shield and said she was going to rush at me. I was determined to fight as hard as I could. I wasn't going to make it easy for her.

Ernie was right. She blazed from the corner with such a furious attack that my head guard catapulted straight off and dangled from my ear. The referee took me back to Tony again, who re-juiced my head.

The first round earned me a bloody nose as I walked onto punch after punch. I had, since leaving Cleto, concentrated hard on improving my non-existent footwork, but had yet to get to the next level of moving my head. I hadn't been at Gelligaer long enough to learn any real ringcraft. Voices floated around and disappeared like bursting bubbles. I could sometimes hear the trainers yelling instructions to me. Sometimes I could hear the crowd as they "oohed" and "aahed" as my head was knocked back time and again. Onwards I marched after her, punching back. When the bell went, Tony wiped away the blood with a towel and I choked on the water he gave me, unable to breathe through my nose.

By the second round it was apparent even to my colleagues standing at the very back of the room that my nose was bleeding like crazy. I began to worry that they would stop the fight.

It's hard work in there. Imagine fighting someone underwater because that's what it feels like. The adrenaline robs you of air. It's why fighters train so relentlessly at all levels. Old timers, they call it wind. You had to have good wind in the old days or you were finished. In Gelligaer it was called blowing up. If a fighter has blown up, then he's too out of breath to carry on.

My breathing settled down halfway through the second round. My nose was even worse though. I could imagine how bad it looked as the girl with the fringed shorts rammed consecutive straight punches into my greasy, red face. I was grateful to the referee for not stopping it. Someone in the audience was concerned about all the blood and waved at the ref. He said I was fine to continue and told me to hold my hands higher. Relieved, I pummelled afresh, battling desperately to avoid defeat. He could see I wasn't going to stop. I took punishment, rallied, then took more punishment and rallied again. The look of confidence on my opponent's face was replaced with one of blood-stained confusion – she was covered in my blood too. Vicky seemed to be surprised that I was still fighting. My face must have looked like a raspberry cheesecake but instinct told me it wasn't permanent damage. By the end of the final round I wore a marinated mask of thick crimson, which had spattered everyone in the front row.

When the bell rang Vicky gave me a hug and smiled. I was smiling too, through the sticky stream, relieved and proud that I had got through it.

"Sorry Tony," I mumbled into the towel as he wiped my face.

"Don't be silly," he said. "You were brilliant!"

I picked up my trophy and faced the obligatory photograph. What I wanted most was a drink. My throat was burning after fighting in the smoky room but I'd had quite enough of being choked with water. Alana popped her head round the changing room door and handed me a pint of diet coke, saying her mother had bought it for me. I could have cheered. Someone came over with a plate of food too. I wanted to drink and wash and eat all at the same time.

I wanted the girls from work to see I was ok so I disappeared off to the toilets to clean up. One of Vicky's friends was in there and helped me get wads of toilet tissue. I wetted it and pressed it to my swollen face. She stayed and chatted for a bit. She had enjoyed the fight but gloated a little.

"You know, Vicky hasn't fought anyone for a while but she still won easy."

"Yeah, any more tissue back there?"

I wondered if my friends would ever get to console the

loser. My nose was getting better but still trickled blood. I reckoned having a runny nose made it look worse.

Making my way back through the crowd was a slow process. People were grabbing me, patting me on the back and shaking my hand. People I did and didn't know were all offering advice, how well I did, how brave I was, how much heart I had shown. A lot of people made a fist and tapped their hearts when I went past. I had smiles for all of them but did think it was a bit weird, seeing as how I'd lost.

I returned to my colleagues declaring that, despite the mess, I was fine. It was then I heard Vicky and I being called for the 'Fight of the Night' award. I went back for my trophy, so overjoyed that I refused to put it down all evening.

People eventually began drifting off and, after saying my goodbyes, I dropped George and Dylan home. I had Dylan hold my trophy for me as he made himself comfortable in the back of Baby.

"One day you'll let me hold your trophies," I prophesied, "you'll have millions of them."

He held the trophy above his head and gave it a shake.

What a fight, I thought, as I got in. Then I shivered. The storage heaters had jettisoned the last of their heat. I ran a bath, listening to the hot tap thundering away as steam drifted as far as the kitchen. I bathed quickly and, smearing condensation from the bathroom mirror, I examined my face. I looked tired. My nose was shiny and tight where it was swollen. I soaked a cotton wool ball in Witch Hazel and dabbed it over the developing bruise. I pressed my fingers to each side of the bridge, and felt it smart.

At least I didn't make it easy for her, I thought.

I unpacked my bag and dumped my kit in the laundry basket, I placed my trophies on the table and made a cup of tea. I felt lonely. I wanted someone to talk to. I switched on the TV and flicked through the channels. Nothing on. Still cold, I dragged my quilt off the bed, wrapped it round me and shuffled back to the sofa. I stared emptily at the TV's late night rubbish. When the tears came, they were swollen with tiredness.

CHAPTER NINE

There was a diamond hardness in the sunlight that cut through the train windows. Fay chattered away to her friend Diane as Jill and I sat separately and squinted at the forms.

"If you don't do it right the court will just send it back and it'll take even longer. You have to fill out that box there, and that there... and sign here and don't forget to attach your cheque."

Again she pointed with a biro to the parts I had to sign.

"You're a star Jill. I couldn't have afforded a solicitor!"

"What's she up to now?" Diane asked Fay.

"Getting a divorce isn't she. Jill's been helping her do the forms as they come in 'cos Jill used to work in family."

"A divorce? She's getting divorced on the train?" Diane doubled over and the seat shook with her laughter. "Divorced on the train!"

Jill waved a hand to get her attention. A few passengers chuckled.

"Diane, if you're going to laugh like that, do it in someone else's office for goodness sake... I can't hear myself think."

They were raucous as they meandered single file up

the aisle approaching their stop. I could still hear Diane at the other end of the carriage.

"Getting divorced on the train... I ask you."

"I'll send you my bill," Jill shouted.

The Decree Absolute came through on May 19, 2005, which had, incidentally, been my wedding day in 2000.

CHAPTER TEN

Fay caressed the nodding freesia petals in the Mother's Day bouquet as we rocked into the tunnel. Fay was good with her mum; so caring. I wanted the same relationship with mine.

"She's Mam," Fay said in that snapped speech she had, "and she hasn't much family around. I don't want to think about going to the Isle of Wight until she's taken care of. She wants me to go though, she's told me and Daniel that, but no way. Flat out, *no*.

"Thing is, she doesn't have a huge family. Mam never really knew her dad, he died in the coal mine when she was small. Terrible, terrible... Did I tell you about that? No? Well, on the day he died, what they did is, they called at her house to tell her mam. Only her mam had had a baby, her little sister, see.

"So there she was at the door, holding her newborn, and she invited them in. Well, they told her right there that there had been an accident and her husband was dead. With the shock... with the awful shock of it, she dropped the baby."

Fay's infant aunt had slipped through her grandmother's numbed fingers. Too late... no time to catch the child with a desperate lunge... and how time had stood still that day! Horror compounded horror as the infant was rushed to the local hospital. She survived for two weeks before joining her father. Two generations were carried on slumped shoulders to the cemetery.

Fay smoothed her fringe from her eyes with two fingers and smiled, but her eyes remained locked for a few seconds longer on the past.

"That's why I *always* say when you get wind of bad news, never have anything in your hands, never be on your feet! I'll always look after her – she's had it hard and she's always smiling. Have I told you about her and the Cointreau."

That's what I loved about the valleys. People included you in their joys and sorrows. They'd share anything with you. Tony and the trainers, they made you feel like family. George's blackberry wine and his presents of apple pies or pancakes; it was generous. George now, he'd had it tough, but he was always giving... always giving and laughing.

Later, at the gym, Ernie brought me in copies of *Boxing News* and pointed out the women's write-ups, or he'd circle around them with a pen, as if he were job hunting. I needed the inspiration. I was getting stale.

"I'd hold the pads for you, like Tony does, but I can't, like." Ernie said. "It's the emphysema. A couple of minutes on the pads and I'd be gasping."

"No worries," I said. "There's plenty of bags."

I had assumed that Ernie just liked fixing up and cleaning and that his job didn't include holding pads. I forgot that it's a workout in itself. Edward and I used to hold the pads for Cleto, to check out his power. It was awesome and exhausting. In my time in boxing I never came across anyone who hit harder. Three minutes of trying not to have your arms ripped from your sockets and you'd be damp with sweat. Although there are few people who punch like Cleto, it's hard work on the arms and shoulders.

My sparring partners had vanished. Alana had an evening job and a couple of my other sparring partners had changed gyms. I skirted the outside of the ring: growing repetitive, feeling like an understudy might in a play where the actors never got sick. I stopped concentrating so much, or improving areas of poor technique. Each day it seemed I talked more and punched a little less. The rounds were mechanical; the same movements on the same bags. It became a habit I loved, but ceased to think about.

Summertime is the closed season in boxing, but the gym stayed open four days a weeks for people like me. I had nothing better to do. The windows, stretched full on their hinges to stave off the bread-oven heat, let in the sound of laughter: of bikes skidding on gravel and balls being kicked. In drifted the smell of charcoal, onions and burgers. A few streets away, Mr Creemy chimed *Just one Cornetto*. At around 7pm, my fellow stragglers and I would leave the baking shed and stumble, blinking, into the sunlight.

Driving home, as the heat lifted and the sky turned the colour of smoked salmon, I longed for the season to start again. It was too quiet. There wasn't much to read in *Boxing News*. I scoured the library for books on sports nutrition as my unhealthy eating habits were leaving me exhausted and not much thinner. I tried yoga and, half hearted, I leafed through one or two self-help books.

I wanted to be surrounded by my fellow-fighters and

trainers. I wished for the damp weather: when they'd light the gas fires, keep the door closed, and the kettle would be doing as many rounds as I did.

A new girl turned up at the gym a few weeks before the season re-opened. I paid Kathy little attention, but the rest of the trainers and boxers did. She was as thin as a catwalk model and must have been at least six foot tall. A pale girl, she wore her ash-blonde hair in a pony-tail and loved her labels. Kathy also claimed to be on first name terms with Rachel Cleaver and her famous trainer, Victor.

As I was making tea for Dai and Tony after my training she strutted over and looked down at me.

"Alright kiddo?" she said, "Mine's two sugars."

In silence I made the tea and pushed a cup towards her.

She talked up her boxing ability and the Rachel Cleaver connection in a manner that would have been applauded by Don King. Alana and I distanced ourselves from the hip-rolling, swaggering bravado of our new friend. Kathy wasn't bad in the ring though. Her height helped her, although there was something coltish in her movements with her being so tall. She sometimes reminded me of a foal learning to stand when she was in the ring with Alana.

Only a few weeks later, as I entered the gym, Ernie bustled towards me wearing a smile warmer than his Arran knit and holding a rolled-up Friday edition of *Boxing News*. His hands slurred it flat to iron out the pages. A women's boxing Welsh squad training session was going to take place on the first weekend of October, at the Welsh Institute of Sport, Sophia Gardens in Cardiff. Phil Jones, National Coach of the Welsh Amateur Boxing

Associaton had written that times were changing and it was 'Wales' turn to prepare for the international stage'. Underneath that, however, was a scathing article by a guy called Colin Pickle who had been picked as team coach. The article assured the reader that the women would only be undertaking light exercises and no sparring. Colin didn't agree with women's boxing and said the squad was an example of 'political correctness gone mad'.

Ernie said they'd already phoned up and put the three of us down to go: Alana, Kathy and me. I didn't know what to make of it. It was too good to be true.

We went to Sophia Gardens together. Alana and I were kind of nervous, the way you feel before an actual fight. We wondered how many girls would be there? What would the sparring be like? How high would the standard be? Kathy looked bored. Complaining of an ankle injury, she ruefully rubbed her foot, then stuck her chin in the air as if she couldn't care less.

The first girl boxer we met, as the rooms were allocated by Phil Jones, was Hayley from Merthyr. She was like someone on a constant caffeine-high; quick moving, quick tempered, quick witted. She spoke fast and funny. She was as alert as a pup and kept doing loud impressions of her dog. She knew Alana from football matches and the two of them were suddenly inseparable. They were given a room to share. I was pleased not to be with them as I couldn't have stood the barking.

I recognised Josie, who had fought Alana the night I boxed Vicky. I felt the relief of the first day of school when you realise you know the kid three desks down in a room full of strangers. Josie said she had read an article in the *South Wales Argus*, written by Colin Pickle saying he wasn't going to let any of us do any sparring. I told her he had written the same in *Boxing News* and we wondered what sort of Women's Boxing Team coach he'd make if there was no sparring and he didn't think any of us should be there.

When Phil Jones made his opening speech there were fourteen girls of various ages and size. We looked hopeful. On the opposite side of the room was a line of teenage boys. We would be sharing the gym with them while the coaches tried to work out what they had with us.

Phil's jaw was tight as he squarely appraised his audience and welcomed us. He gave us a list of the coaches' credentials, including his own substantial qualities as National Coach. When he introduced Colin a twitch of furtive glances swept along the line of girls. "The name of the game," Phil said, "is to think ahead to the Olympic Games 2012." He said he hoped some of us would keep up with the boys but he wanted us to do as much as we could and try our best.

Colin Pickle stepped forward and I took him in. In his vest, Colin's arms, shoulders and chest, tanned to conker colour, were covered with a grey fuzz more like new mould spores on an old red pepper than body hair. Beneath the fluff ran tattoos faded as Italian frescoes on peeling plaster although they sure as hell weren't done by Michelangelo. His claim to fame was that he'd sparred with both Henry Cooper and Joe Erskine. I didn't like Colin, and it wasn't just because when I passed him earlier on he'd whispered, '*Obvious bleedin' lesbian*' in Phil's ear – pointing to a girl who looked no different from the rest of us. As he talked, Colin's stained teeth bit up and down like two rows of Sugar Puffs. There was something of the sixties London gangster about him. I was sure he would have happily worked for the Cardiff equivalent of the Kray twins, or, saying that, Colin Pickle might have *been* the Cardiff Kray for all I knew. He reiterated what he'd said in the papers.

"You'll have to prove me wrong," he finished.

After a weigh-in we were taken into the grounds for a run. The boys were told to go around three times and the girls once. I looked at Josie and wondered whether she would continue regardless and do three. If she did, then I would too. We set off and it was obvious that Josie was set on keeping up with the boys. I aimed to stay level with her. On we raced, jumping the puddles, as the other girls slowed their pace and jogged. Some quickly grew tired and walked.

When Josie slowed after the first lap, and I pulled up at her heels, she asked whether she could continue with the boys. She was told no. We were to use the boxing gym while the boys were still running. It made sense, I suppose, but we wanted to prove Colin wrong, like he said we should. Such a strange boxing weekend, I thought.

In the gym it got stranger. Colin told us to put on wraps and bag gloves and said that we had to wear our gum shields, even though we weren't sparring.

"What's the bet it's so he doesn't have to listen to us talking about nail varnish and lipstick," I said, before I put in the hard plastic shield and chewed it nervously.

"What's with the no sparring?" someone whispered.

"Just do as you're told," shouted Colin. "I've got bloody chest hair older and wiser than you lot."

No, I didn't like him at all. He was the kind of man you couldn't reason with. I knew he'd be impossible to get round. I got the impression even Phil Jones didn't like him much.

Later, Phil came back and announced officially we

were going to be the Women's Welsh Boxing Squad. Josie was named as team captain. As she took us for a stretching session I applauded his decision. She was easily the fittest and, having sparred with her once myself, and received a black eye for my efforts, I knew first hand she was accomplished. Furthermore, she was strong enough to stand up to Colin.

The training in the gym was hard, but the long breaks in between were worse because they were mentally draining. That evening, Hayley and Alana press-ganged a number of us into playing basketball against a group of teenagers they'd met. I didn't know the rules. I shuffled into the sports hall feeling small under the fluorescent lights. I wasn't used to groups of girls. It was a playground hangover.

I did my best to avoid the ball at all costs and watched from the edges as they screeched and ducked each other. In the end I gave up and slunk off to bed. I tried to sleep, but I was preoccupied with endless questions, getting no answers in the dark; questions about belonging, about being invisible, and about fitting in.

The Sunday weigh-in was at 7.15am in Josie's room and I was 61.04kg. The breaks in between training weren't so long. From the balcony we could see into the main hall where the gymnastic trials were taking place. The Women's Boxing Squad couldn't have been more of a contrast. I would have loved to have been that graceful. We felt protective as they danced and leapt in front of the judges, who looked on with faces of stone. We gasped when their hoops or ribbons fluttered from their fingers. There's always one though.

"I bet she drops that bat'n!" Stacy said.

"Batt-*en*," corrected Hayley, with her strong Merthyr accent. "Will you stop putting a jinx on her. Frickin' leave her alone, she's doing ok, see."

A second later the gymnast dropped her batten.

"Bloody bitch – that's you, that is!" stormed Hayley. "See, plus they're dead fucking tight those judges an they say, yeah, she did it great, and well... the thing is, see, but her fucking finger stuck out a bit when she landed and her foot was pointing a tiny bit to the left – *take off ten points!*"

We laughed as the next gymnast took to the floor.

Alana watched, open-mouthed. "D'you see that! Frickin' hell, she do put her legs back and flick that hula hoop with the tops of her feet. It's not *right*! What I want to do, see, is get one of them by the ankles and swing them round. Yeah, 'cos I bet they're light as feathers!"

I reckoned Alana was one of those kids who pulled the wings off dragonflies.

"She's so good she makes you forget that her costume's crap!" I chipped in. Even if we didn't make it to the 2012 Olympic Boxing Squad, there was always the Olympic Gymnastic Commentary Team.

We sprinted like an African stampede, did touch sparring so they could assess footwork, and went through more fitness tests. The President of the Amateur Boxing Association arrived and Colin introduced him as "someone who also shares my distaste for women's boxing". The President and Phil Jones laughed off Colin's remark and on that note we were sent home, after being advised that the next squad was near the end of October.

As Michael finished dictating, I had a call from Tony. He asked whether I could box Alana that evening as there was a show on which was short of fighters. I told him I'd be there as soon as I could. Two hours later I was in the gym saying hello to Tony and Ernie, who were leaning on the corner ring ropes.

"Can I warm up?" I asked, feeling stiff from sitting all day.

"No. Have a cup of tea and a sit down."

I slumped onto a seat as their conversation circled above me. Tony pulled on his flat cap and sucked the life out of his cigarette. He always smoked them like that, with his cigarette dangling from the left corner of his mouth so he could talk out of the centre.

"...Yeah, well," he said to Ernie, "Colin Pickle phoned about this show tonight. There's loads dropped out. The whole night's turning out to be a real stinker by the sound of it. Colin said to me, 'Tony, I'm embarrassed to have to ask but any chance I could have the girls?' See, *embarrassed* to have to ask."

Tony tapped my shoulder. "See Liz, Colin was embarrassed to ask for you and Alana."

First he doesn't think women should box, I thought, and then he's embarrassed to have to ask for me. *An embarrassment!* And I raced over here at short notice. Oh, and I bet he'll put us on first: before they've got their drinks; when everyone is still at the bar with their backs to the ring. It's over... it's finished. If the Women's Team Coach thinks you're an embarrassment, it's time to hang up your gloves.

The fight was at Llanharan Rugby Club, an all-purpose community hall, which was already full as Alana and I dropped down our bags.

"You're on first," Tony said, and I nodded.

Gloved-up at the side of the ring, I listened in confusion to the instructions of the Llanbradach Gym corner-man.

"Now you listen to me, *you*. As long as you have fun, always do your best and work hard. Never look a gift horse in the mouth and you should always count your blessings and be good. Yes, be *good*. Tony said you live in Pontllanfraith. I used to live by there; just round the corner from The Plough. You know The Plough? Nice house too, nice area. So anyway, always be true to yourself and genuine; and be good, and work hard."

He let go of the gentle grip on my elbow and waved to one of the judges.

"She's single if you want a date. Go to the pictures, like!"

I doubted it would make a difference to the result.

Alana was announced from All Saints, Caerphilly, which raised the heads of the All Saints gym who hadn't heard of her. They had to pretend she was from a different gym because Gelligaer v Gelligaer isn't encouraged.

If I'm being honest it was a lousy fight; three boring rounds of boxing but, hell, I thought sourly, give the crowd what they want – the men.

The following day I turned up at the gym preoccupied with the fight, and squad. I didn't understand what Ernie was trying to say at first as he attempted a repair to the snapped elastic on the floor-to-ceiling reaction ball.

"Liz, if you'd been in here yesterday, you would have cried, I'm telling you now. You would have been in tears and gone home."

What was this about now? My performance? Was Colin angry with me? Was Gangsta Grampa Pickle going to break my kneecaps?

"I haven't seen anything that bad in years and years. You

would have cried, I'm telling you. What a thing to happen!"

"What is it? What's happened?"

"That Kathy came in, and... she went over to Rachel Cleaver's gym for sparring, and... well, Rachel Cleaver broke her nose! Her face is a total mess and she's got two of the nastiest black eyes I've seen in years."

The elastic twanged out of Ernie's hand, whip-cracked the ceiling, and then hung limp. He rolled his eyes.

Surprised, I sat on the ringside leaning back on my hands, until I realised that my fingers had spread through explosions of half-dry dark red droplets, like a handful of trodden blackberries. I wiped my hands on my trousers and held the ball in place for Ernie.

"That's not from her is it?" I asked him, nodding towards the blackening splashes.

"No, she's not bleeding now, that's that kid Kyle. That kid's hooter is like a frickin' tap, eh Dai?"

"Oh aye, he's a bleeder all right. He needs to get a couple of pounds off but bleeding's not the way to do it. Is he telling you about Kathy?" Dai asked. "You should've seen her, *phewee*, what a mess. She's hoping to go pro, see. I've had Rachel Cleaver in here a few times and... good as gold but *phewee*... she broke Kathy's nose alright."

"How's she doing?" I asked.

"She said Rachel told her she can go for sparring this Friday and she wants to go. She's insane!"

I wondered whether Kathy would make it to squad with a broken nose. I started to wonder if I would either, with Colin's embarrassment comment churning away in my insides. By the following Wednesday I didn't want to go squad training. I'd lost confidence and worried that the effort I'd put in amounted to nothing more than my making an enormous fool of myself in the world of boxing.

For the first time at the gym I turned up without my training gear. Tony sensed something was wrong.

"I'd best put the kettle on," I said.

"We're out of tea bags, Babes. What's up?"

"I've got a problem Tony."

I felt ashamed. I couldn't think how to tell them boxing was over. I didn't know if I could leave it anyway. The explanation slopped out, as if from a full jug into a shot glass.

Tony replied that if he thought I was wasting my time he'd tell me so. He told me to do one last squad and see how I felt then. Later George, who had listened to the conversation with a wry smile, had a quiet talk to me about boxing.

"You got Fight of the Night," he reminded me quietly. "It's in your blood, you know. Everyone feels like you do now at some point, I know I have. But they always come back. Often it's not even a matter of choice."

Why was it so like religion?

I didn't need to tell anyone about my change of heart after speaking to George and Tony. Anyone could see it and I went to squad that weekend so much happier.

I shared a room with the recuperating Kathy, whose black eyes brought her an endless stream of reprimands about sparring with professional fighters. I felt for her as her bravado was shredded by her constant explanations and attempts to shrug off lectures.

"Rachel did me a favour breaking my nose you know, I mean, if I can take a punch from her, I can take a punch from anyone. She's just toughened me up, see, physically and mentally, and I can take on anyone. I might even do your weight, *fatty*."

But she hadn't been toughened up by having her nose broken. Rachel had given every one of Kathy's opponents in the ring a weakness to aim for.

The second squad was much harder than the first and opened with a surprisingly optimistic look at the following year, when we might get a chance to go abroad and fight. It would start with a Sweden trip for four of us in January.

Vicky, my third opponent, and partner in Fight of the Night, turned up this time. She said Phil persuaded her to come along. It was well known that Josie, Vicky, Alana, and Hayley were the best female boxers in Wales. Those girls could counter, slip and switch hit with the best of them.

"My nose remembers you," I said to Vicky.

"I've still got some of your blood on my head guard. It was everywhere."

We heaved our aching muscles through more National Service-style exercises and even got the chance to do some sparring, as Colin was away in Finland with Josie. We headed to the cafeteria for lunch. Smells of crisp, buttery jacket potatoes and curry and rice drew me in. Everything I wanted was loaded with carbohydrate and I was one of the few scoffing it down. I wished I had everyone else's control, but I couldn't resist.

Outside of squad no one cooked for me and I rarely went out to dinner so it was a wonderful, comforting thing to pick up a brown tray and cutlery, and choose whatever I wanted. I pondered over the steaming silver lids of the hot bay as the dinner lady expounded what was on. It was all free. Squad paid for breakfast, lunch and dinner. There were such yoghurts, the toffee ones were wonderful, as well as the selection of fruit for dessert. You could get tea refills as often as you wanted. I would've fought Ricky Hatton if it meant being looked after like that on a regular basis.

I'd just finished in the bathroom when, on the way out of our room, I noticed Kathy's gym schedule in the bin. I hadn't got a copy and so I gingerly pulled it out. Underneath the schedule sat her unopened sandwiches. I covered them up again hastily.

The last exercise before our dismissal on the Sunday was a weights competition. We had to stand facing forward with our arms stretched out to the sides like wings and hold the weights at shoulder height until our arms dropped. The trainer stressed that the boys' squad record was set at an impressive six minutes, so if we did anything over three it would be great.

In my head I left the gym. I imagined myself on Barry Island beach. It was late afternoon and I leant both my arms on the warm sea wall overlooking the yellow-ochre ribbing in the long stretch of sand. I simply stood there toasting in the sunlight, looking out at the silver sea. I thought about Tony and George and our last conversation. The sunshine got hotter and burnt. My eyes narrowed with pain and still I stood against that burning wall and didn't move.

Torment wrenched me back to the gym and I had been at the beach for five minutes. Everyone except me and one other girl had given up. She was being distracted by remembering the names of Quality Streets.

"Strawberry Cream, *argh*, Toffee*eee* Penny... *urrgggghhh*." Her arms fell.

The group closed in on me, realising I was going for the record. I heard their clapping and encouragement, as if from a long way away.

That's about the time it got bad. It was a world away from Barry Island. For a start it was foggy and getting more so. The weights began trying to shake loose from my trembling fingers. I clung on tighter. The convulsive twitching spread up my arms and I struggled to focus. Everything was pain. The figures in the mist in front of me could have been girls or gorillas for all I knew. I squinted damply at them as beads of sweat trickled down my face like tears.

One of the trainers goaded the crowd.

"She can't do six minutes, *SHE JUST CAN'T!*"

"Do it Liz. Do it!" a load of shapeless apes hooted and screeched.

I'm going to faint, I thought.

The sixth minute ticked past to a thundering cheer, and I let the weights clunk to the floor.

I'd done it. We were dismissed.

A rough hand clamped around my wet neck and I found it was the guest trainer from up Merthyr way. He'd already given me all the details of his coal mine-related emphysema but his claim wasn't with Don Rankin and Marshall.

"I knew Howard Winstone," he wheezed. "Saw him train; just saw the same in you." He tapped his chest with his fist. "You know what I mean, don't you? You don't see that hunger so much nowadays. These girls are good, some of 'em outstanding, but not one could do what you did. You can't give someone that, they've got it or they haven't... but you don't see it so much anymore."

He handed me a scribbled rag of paper with his number on.

"Call me if you need sparring. I wish to God I'd had

you from a kid. Dream come true that is. What a trainer always wants... that hunger... that heart."

On Monday I didn't tell my trainers the specifics, but my smile said all they needed to know.

"See, I told you," said George. "It's in your blood."

CHAPTER ELEVEN

The last Wednesday in October I hit the street running, not long after 4.50am. I jogged gently down St Ivor's Road towards the Sirhowy Trail. I'd started doing hill sprints on the A472, between the lamp posts. I flew through the sprints from glow to glow, measuring the distance – past one, two, three lamp posts and then I bounced along, slowing my breathing down until passing a final fourth. Then I began the cycle again. I felt great. I was running with the wind, pushing harder and harder, fleet and buoyant. I raced on, counting off those glowing orange balls: hands clenched, shoulders relaxed, elbows and knees like cod-liver-oiled pistons, pumping joyously. I did more sprints than usual, feeling clear and free.

Small things made that morning. The hot water was just the perfect temperature for a shower. I opened the new box of Bran Flakes. My hair dried just right.

I checked out of the window and saw a soft drizzle had begun. I took down my black cotton raincoat. My tea was too hot to rush it so I blew on it, picking up the remote control to turn off the TV. The local news was beginning. I was surprised to recognise a night shot of

Bryn Terrace, showing the street name of a side road, Oakdale Rise. The low rail that ran along the Bryn Terrace path gleamed in the drizzle. I'd know that road anywhere, I thought, even in the dark. In actual fact I knew it better in the dark. It didn't occur to me that the pictures were live, that the camera man was only two streets away, peering through his lens as it clouded with morning moisture.

I had run up Bryn Terrace every day since moving to Pontllanfraith, exactly a year before. It was only since squad that I'd decided to do sprinting in the mornings as well. I had, as with Roath Park, seen all four seasons scudding past and I'd been embraced by all weathers on my route. My regular five mile run was well loved and well worn. It had its own touchstone, my own place to nod to mentally as I passed. To make a salute.

Running is lonely of course, and sometimes, when the morning feels darker, when shadows are deeper and cars slow suspiciously on their journey, it's good to have a friend. In Cardiff it was the lake itself I said hello to. In Pontllanfraith it was George Wise's house on Oakdale Rise. It was better than the lake. If I broke a bone, if I was attacked, if I was in trouble, I could go to George's. A whole parade of 'ifs' were ticked off and fell away fast – easy as sprinting past lamp posts – just because of that inward "morning George" as I ran past his house. I told him once that I ran past every morning, but he hadn't been listening. I know this because after I got to know him better I realised he would have been unhappy to think of me out alone. He would have berated me with a grandfatherly grin, tucking his hands into the front pockets of his caramel leather coat.

I smiled when I saw his street sign on the news. I'll have

to tell him that his street was on TV, I thought. The news reader's voice said, "George and his wife, Grace... " my head swam as the voice went on " ...died after their car was hit head on in a collision with a lorry."

My senses left me like a collapsing star. I felt them crush together, implode. My knees went and I staggered, dropping the remote control and the cup I was still holding. Fay was right, I thought, as tears dropped towards the tea.

"Never have anything in your hands when you get bad news. Never be on your feet!"

My hand found my collar: I couldn't breathe. The news item finished. I needed to rewind it or replay it but it went on, uncaring to another place, other lives. I couldn't believe what I thought they'd said. I grabbed a handful of tissues and raced out into the street, head pounding.

Shock left my breath thin, but I ran as fast I could. I thought of the lie the news had broadcast and, strangely, of the terrible story Fay had told me that day on the train.

I tried to control my tear-stained panic as I tore past two peering early commuters at the bus stop. Did they know? Had they heard the news? I wanted to ask but I didn't. I didn't want to stop. I prayed that I would get to his street and it would be silent; they would all still be asleep, safe.

There was the fence-rail, looping up towards Blackwood and George's street. I ran up to the policeman outside George's house. The road was lit by a rolling stream of blue light.

"Are you a friend or family?" he asked as I approached.

I choked out the word "friend". It didn't say enough. I wanted to say, selfishly, that I was someone who needed him.

"Is it true?" I asked, stupidly. Had he said no I would

have believed him regardless; I could have believed it was a false alarm.

He nodded. I got the feeling that he had been told not to say too much.

I cried into a scrambled egg of clenched tissue.

"Is there anywhere you can go? Anyone who can stay with you?" the policeman asked.

"Yes," I said, but inside I said no, not anymore.

I got to work in the end. I sat on the train trying not to blink, staring out of the window so others wouldn't see. In work I stumbled a shaky explanation to Michael and tried hard to control the panic in my voice. Seeing how distressed I was I was sent home, compassionate leave, like punishment – to sit in my empty flat by myself.

I went back to Blackwood and ordered a bouquet of white flowers. In the lashing rain I walked back to George's house. I gave my name to the policeman as I placed the flowers beneath George's window. His family had been, and their flowers and loving messages leant for support against the wet, brown bricks.

In the evening I went up to the gym and sat in a daze on the dirty ring steps. Dai came in and looked devastated. His eyes were glassy and ringed with purple. Harry nodded at him and whispered in my ear, "When Dai phoned me about George, he was in a right state... he wasn't making sense at all." Harry shook his head and sighed.

It appeared that George and Grace had been driving back late at night from the Heads of the Valleys. No one could really say how the accident had happened; it was such a lonely stretch of road. All we knew was that, though it seemed to make no sense, they had gone.

I took the next day off too and spent the morning cleaning the gym. I started well, vacuuming the ring and sweeping the floor; heating the water to clean the tables and mirrors, but it was the wrong place to take my mind off it. Everywhere I looked in the emptiness held memories. The shadows drove me out.

I went food shopping instead, but I had to go home at some point. I was heartbroken. I wanted to speak to my mum and so I called her on the payphone. She sounded busy.

"I'm just about to get my hair done so I can't stay long."

"I know, but he was good to me... " I was crying.

"Well, that's what you get for spending the day by yourself. You've got no one to blame but yourself. You should have gone to work," she said.

I put the phone down on her, but I was unable to leave it there, thinking of George and Fay and the aunt she never knew, of loss and families.

I called her back.

"I don't know why... I don't know why I can't... say things," Mum said. "I do care about you, you know that don't you?" It was her turn to cry.

"Sure."

I dried my tears. I laughed with her and gently mocked the fact that she never had much patience with me. Inside, however, I wasn't laughing. Inside, I didn't understand them at all. I was lost. I felt the whole bloody lot of us were useless. A family that wasn't a family.

I went to the mountain before the gym. I had a strange, strong feeling I should go there, go and say goodbye to George. It seemed as good a place as any; open and private at the same time. I needed to be alone. High up, I sploshed sadly down the ribbon of flooded lane between high-spined hedges. It had been overcast all day, grey and still, but as I got higher my path was barred by sunlight, cutting through the bruised clouds and stretched shadows, tight as violin strings. The silver birches lining the path were stark in the late sun, their white skin studded with black iron nails: stigmata. Everywhere there were bramble thorns.

On the open mountain I stopped by an old, brown-stone wall. I leant on the stones and looked out over the valley. The sun splashed across the soaked fields, colouring them and turning the rain to diamonds. Two glorious rainbows appeared. I scrabbled up the wall, knocking off fern and moss in clumps, and sat on the top to get the best view of the unbelievably bright arcs. In the distance three gulls traced their way above the hills, their wing-backs reflecting light, silver arrows moving across the blackening clouds. It felt as if the world was deliberately trying to push back at the bleak-ness inside me, to beat it down, wash it away. I sat there until the rainbows faded and the rain started again. Then I put up my hood and headed for home. I tried to keep the picture in my head but by the time I got home grief had weakened it, diluted it into something greyer and watered down. By the funeral the following Tuesday, the memory was even paler, a scene set hard into mother of pearl.

Although the funeral didn't start until 11.30am, the church and the hall next door were full by 10.30. The sky hung coldly, low and gloomy. I turned up alone, as usual, and edged towards the waiting crowd. I hated why I was there. I hated the fact that one of my scarcely worn black shoes had become unbuckled and my tights were scratchy and stiff. Everything about this day was wrong and wretched.

I put up a hand of recognition to Ernie, who was

pallbearer to George along with Dai, Harry, and Tony. Later, Ernie and I managed to get seats in the church hall where a crackling intercom was wired from the church service to us and a car park full of people. As I stood up and choked out the first few lines of *Amazing Grace* I saw through the bowed heads into the car park. Outside it could have been a painting by Seurat: a landscape speckled with black umbrellas and hundreds of fleshy flecks, faces intent and solemn. They came and came, those mourners, and through my tears the tiny white dots of collars and hankies against still and sombre black coats blurred into a whole night sky of respect and love.

The service ended and the throng marshalled itself slowly from the church to the cemetery in Bedwellty. Later, many of those at the funeral met at Blackwood Rugby Club, where the talk was of George and his family, and then, inevitably, boxing.

Ernie started over his water as if he'd remembered something.

"You never got to try his blackberry wine."

"He didn't finish it. I helped him collect the blackberries only last month up by the school."

"I've got a bottle left over from last year. I can't drink much anymore. He'd have wanted you to have it anyway. Make sure you drink it till you pass out. It's what he would've wanted. Raise a glass to him, like."

"I will do, thanks Ernie."

A few hours later, when Tony wiped his beery mouth with the back of a cold freckled hand, drawling that I looked gorgeous, I knew the world had begun to breathe again.

CHAPTER TWELVE

They demolished the squalid slum housing of Newtown, Cardiff, in November 1966 but that's where my grandfather obstinately ended his days anyway. He actually lived in Tremorfa, but a comfort blanket of nostalgia had cloaked him and his tired, tweedy armchair. In the evenings, he warmed wiry knees by the fireside and disappeared back into memories of his childhood home. He wrote long poems about Newtown or 'Little Ireland' as some knew it, but in truth they were simply love letters to friends of the past.

Gramps was always well dressed and clean-shaven. I rarely saw him without bits of tissue stuck to his chin. He smelt of shaving foam and Old Spice, but also of cigarettes, damp tea leaves, old coins and tomato plants, the fruits of which clustered in varying degrees of ripeness on his kitchen windowsill. When we called round to see him he would recite rhymes, which came bubbling out of the creaky bellows in his brittle old chest; his Irish pipes out of puff with emphysema. The poems were his literary Embassy Extra Mild.

That's how I knew him on one level. He still played with us and his wrinkled hands would rattle the yellowing dice before they skittled across the board game. Sometimes we'd play gin rummy instead and, for a bit of luck, he'd whisper "Baby needs new shoes," or he'd pretend to be a body builder and flex his bony frame to a tune on the TV until, out of puff again, he would rattle his inhaler.

Still, at the end of the day he always drew back into dreams of his youth. Funny how I always thought of it as the same as us kids being called in for tea after street games, when all the back doors clattered like a round of applause in the dying light.

On another level, I knew him as he was in his photograph, although that was the man I'd never met. That was the young gramps, aged 22, when he won the Welsh vest. He'd written on the photo himself, "*Western Counties Champ 1935-6, Welsh Light-Weight Champion 1936-7.*"

His boxing shorts are home-made in that photograph, cut out of an old cotton bed sheet, but someone has done a painstaking job of embroidering his name, 'Joe Collins,' on the left leg. He fought for Wales in those shorts. His fists are a bunch of big knuckles; a builder's hands. His hair, his trademark, is the typical short back and sides but the fringe is long and curls away from his forehead. His mouth is open a fraction in a determined smile. There was no narrative to accompany the photo, or none that I ever heard anyway. Gramps had been the only storyteller in our family and he'd never mentioned it. It's possible he'd thought boxing would have limited interest to a little girl but I knew him regardless. I identified with him, never mind space and time – just as he had identified with Newtown. He haunted me, the young gramps in the picture, because I knew the boxing came from the same place in me as it came from in him and I knew that we were connected.

It was in my blood.

I'd known George for a little over a year, but it was like losing a grandfather again. The difference was that this time I'd got to know him a little first and understood the true value of him. To lose George and his poor wife – it was too much.

The world was washed out.

Josie James' success on the international stage passed me by that autumn. I had been told that Colin Pickle was abroad with Josie for the Wales v Finland contest. I had acknowledged what an honour it must be to represent your country and this was particularly true in Josie's case. She was the first woman to represent Wales. Nevertheless, it took me a while to realise that life without George was continuing around me, and fast.

Then it sank in. A girl from our squad had gone to Finland and represented Wales in amateur boxing for the first time ever. Double history had been made, both for women and the sport of boxing in Wales. Josie turned in an exceptional performance. She knocked her opponent out in round two. Yet the real significance for me came before she got in the ring.

Josie had on the red Welsh vest.

Everything became clear in an instant. The photograph of Grampy in his Welsh vest and worn-out hotchpotch shorts, and my insatiable need to prove my own worth. What if I could? What if I could get the red vest? What if I could get myself picked to fight for Wales? It felt right. I made it my New Year's resolution.

I knew it wouldn't be easy. I thought about Josie and what she had that enabled her to be the first. She was fitter than me and, even though she had been boxing for only two years, she possessed a natural talent. I thought back to our sparring and how she had taken me apart. In boxing circles, with uncharacteristic politeness, they call it being dismantled. She had all the ringcraft and strategy you could want. Whatever you were supposed to do in boxing, 'punches in bunches', 'head and body', 'dig and move', she did it with an expressive and elastic movement. She could switch hit and she could feint as much as anyone could want.

I promised myself it wasn't impossible. Maybe I would never be as quick as Josie. Yes my head moved a fraction slower, my shoulders were sometimes a bit stiff, and I always put too much weight behind shots, but I was sure there was a boxer in me somewhere as well as a fighter.

If I tried hard, then beneath that fighter's heart of mine there might be a little gracefulness that I could eke out; so important for the snappy point-scoring of amateur boxing.

I was late in the gym one Thursday night and everyone had left except for Tony, Harry, and me. Harry had hung around only to call one of his pro-fighters on his mobile. Tony shut off all the lights apart from the row next to the mirrors and the far end of the ring was in semi-darkness. It was a poignant place when lit candle-low, and the bags hung like folded bats. My bulging kit bag was slung over a shoulder and occasionally I tugged two-handed at the strap, like a bell ringer, as I headed for the door. Harry, finished on the phone, called me back. He unfolded a paper and his reading glasses.

"I forgot to show it to you after... it's here, look."

He held *The Campaign*. I guessed it was the article that 'Don King' Kathy had been interviewed for. Dai had already told me about it, as he scratched his head in confusion. He said the last thing any boxer should do is announce in the papers that they've had their nose broken, unless they wanted every opponent to try to repeat the damage. I read the story and saw, candidly written, *'Kathy, pictured below, is sporting black eyes and a broken nose after a sparring session with the women's world champion in a Swindon gym, but she is more eager than ever because of the incident.'* Next to the words were two photographs of Kathy with her indigo and yellow eye sockets.

"Never listen to Kathy mind..." Harry said as I continued reading, "and go over to Swindon without one of us. Now, I've told Alana... and I told everybody."

"I wouldn't," I assured him.

"Aye, he's right Babes, and I told Kathy the other day... "

"I mean Rachel's alright don't get me wrong, but she's tough and you've got to watch her... because aye... remember Jason Stephens, Tony?"

"Oh aye."

"*Whoa*, she took advantage of Jason Stephens, banged the bloody shit out of him. She's a thug sometimes, and the language on her... have you seen her on TV?"

"Yeah."

"That's nothing... nothing... she'd make a man turn his head away... that bad!

"And she doesn't even know how hard she hits. Tony, how many times have you seen another boy's legs going and the one lad doesn't even know he's done it? But if that Kathy girl hasn't learnt her lesson now I'm going to... well, you know she had to have an X-ray on her cheek?"

Tony shut off the lights and only the doorway was illuminated.

"I didn't know that," Tony said.

"You didn't know that did you? Well, that's not sparring... that's fighting!"

Harry and Tony hovered while I finished reading. I learnt that Kathy was running in the mountains twice a day, and was on a strict diet for a tour with the Welsh Women's Boxing Squad to Sweden. She hadn't said anything about being picked. Lucky thing, I thought. If Kathy was going to Sweden that left three places and Alana and Vicky would be going for certain. The coaches had said as much, they were the most experienced girls on squad. That left one place and there were about five girls in addition to myself that could be considered. Slim odds to say the least.

I wasn't the only one to have a new goal.

It wasn't unusual for Michael to phone me six or seven times before 10am.

"Come on down, Collins, I've got a *huge one* down here I want you to help me with."

"I'm on my way."

I spent much of my day ignoring sexual innuendo and running along royal-blue carpeted corridor rather than typing.

"Close the door, quick, I want to ask you about something while you *get them out*," he purred as he pointed to the neat pile of morning post.

I ignored him.

"*Get them out* for the lads," he repeated, amused. "You happy here, Collins?"

"Of course I am."

"Yeah but you're dressed nicely today. You wouldn't be sneaking off to an interview or anything like that now?"

I looked down. It wasn't much different to any other day, brown trousers and a cream cardigan.

"Of course not. I'd never leave you... I'm like Kevin Costner and you're Whitney Houston... you know, in *The Bodyguard*. I'd take a bullet for you boss."

"I don't want to be Whitney Houston but I commend your loyalty."

He'd never really trusted me since I'd gone for an interview with Longman's.

"What did you want to ask me about? And I don't want to hear any questions on Cameron Diaz's jubblies because, yes, I think they've been airbrushed," I said, dropping a pile of post onto *GQ Magazine*.

"I've been thinking of going on a diet and you know about stuff like that."

"That's a great idea – brilliant!" Where had this come from? However it had been inspired it was about time. Chloe and the girls had also noticed his big 'moony' face was getting bigger.

"I need to lose about two stone if I'm honest and I want to know the best way to go about it."

I didn't hesitate. "First off, the girls said you ate seven chocolate digestives in a row yesterday. You want to stop doing that."

"Yeah, they were nice though."

"It's a wonderful idea – really."

I understood why Michael asked me. I ignored the boxes of Sainsbury mini-doughnuts and blanked the Tesco tubs of mini rolls. I never touched anything I didn't prepare at home. I was all self-discipline, but it was only because I couldn't trust myself and the all or nothing relationship I had with food. I had irrational fears when eating in public. I worried that people might take my food. I found it hard to eat if they were talking to me. I couldn't eat while people were in the same room, and I would hide my lunch in my drawer until they were gone.

If caught out, I froze as they leant over my Tupperware.

"Oh, what've you got there then?"

"Nothing... just salad and stuff. Nothing."

"Did you make it yourself? It looks very healthy."

Eating was complicated; a private thing and best undertaken behind closed doors. I was the last person in the world Michael should have talked to.

On the last day in November I noticed a voicemail message on my phone. "It's Tony," said the message, before clicking off. He hated talking to machines. I called him back and he explained he'd heard a rumour that Phil Jones had put Alana and me down for Sweden. I sat there in a day dream – my mobile phone hanging in no-man's-land.

I've always seen life as a fight. I earn things the hard way, with overtime, or with blood and sweat and tears. I get nothing for nothing. Life was a run of sacrifices and skirmishes, and now I was supposed to believe that I could jet off to Sweden and get the red vest. Tony's mistaken, I thought. I refused to take any notice until squad announced the names officially.

But was I being too cynical? If I stopped to think about it, I didn't know anyone else who shared my view that they were in a series of life battles. Happy things happened to people all the time. People were celebrating all over the world. There were weddings, children being born, people falling in love, people being promoted – and it happened all the time. Was it possible that my own attitude might be at fault? Maybe I was too suspicious. I decided to try to be a little more trusting.

I told a couple of my colleagues I might be going to Sweden and it felt wonderful. By the end of the week it was an accepted fact. I glittered with good news. People were pleased for me. I was loaned a guide to Sweden from a girl in accounts who had recently returned from a weekend break there.

At night, however, if that guidebook could have giggled at me from the bedside table, it would have. It lay there, unopened. I felt it was a jinx; a con to make me believe that I had any control. It wasn't just time to slow things down, it was time to backtrack.

The next squad training was in December. I drove Alana down there and met Tony in the foyer; he was one of the guest trainers that weekend. I told him that Kathy had sent me a text saying she had a stomach upset and couldn't make it.

"Babes, *Boxing News* will be crushed," he said.

Perhaps because it was so close to Christmas there were fewer of us, around eleven girls. We arrived in the dance studio to find the small shape of Hayley curled, half asleep, on a crash mat in the middle of the boxing ring. We smiled and sat next to her, waiting as she stretched out.

Following our usual warm-up and weigh-in, we went straight into the morning run. It was another golden day. Panting and thirsty, we raced along the banks of the Taff, its shallow water bubbling over the bronze cobbles like cold ginger beer.

I was the first out of the girls to reach the finish, having kept pace with the boys. There were a couple of sprints to finish the run off and I felt fit.

I was sharing a room with a fourteen-year-old kickboxer called Chelsea. I knew her a little. She had sparred in Gelligaer for a while until her father had been banned from the gym by an angry Tony. I liked Chelsea. She was a pleasant kind of girl, but her father, a thick-set man who lived and breathed in kick boxing t-shirts, lauded his daughter's talent and his own coaching ability until he had few friends left. We all saw it coming – the day he pushed Tony too far. Tony, with raised hackles, had banned Chelsea's dad from the gym. As I flexed my fingers, examining my knuckles which were bleeding and raw, she told me she'd found another boxing gym, but there was no one to spar with. I sympathised with her.

"That looks dead sore," she said, looking at my hand. Rushing to get ready that morning, I'd grabbed an old pair of bag gloves, which had no stuffing left over the knuckles. The ratty old bandages I'd wrapped my hands in offered little protection. I may as well have been smashing the pads with my bare fists. The repetitive pad work that morning removed the skin from the first two knuckles on my right hand. Because of the squad's constant punching drills it wasn't going to have much of a chance to heal. It was an agonising distraction that I hoped would mend itself quickly.

Over dinner Chelsea drew everyone's attention to my hand.

"You want to piss on them," Alana said.

I made to pull down my trousers there at the dinner table. "Get lost," I said. "That's the craziest thing I've ever heard."

"No really, all boxers do it. It toughens up the skin like, when you've got cuts. Let them heal, and then give it a try. I've been lucky I've never had cuts, but the boys in the Bargoed gym do it all the time."

"I'm not fussed myself. Thanks, but I'll try surgical spirit first. Urinating on myself is always a last resort."

Even I had my limits.

An exhausting day dragged into an early evening with a game of basketball. I threw myself into it, still clueless of the rules, and scampered back and forth as tiredness scratched at my efforts.

"Catch it Liz!" someone yelled across the court. I caught the basketball full force – between the eyes.

"Head like a coconut!" I announced, blinking and pride-damaged.

I crept into bed and disturbed Chelsea's viewing of the Audley Harrison v Danny Williams fight by snuffling, wriggling and talking in my sleep. I didn't stay asleep for long though. At some point, the bottom sheet got twisted up and slithered off like a serpent, and I spent the rest of the night sweating on the plastic mattress. The morning couldn't come soon enough... I would find out then whether I was picked for Sweden.

Sparring the next day, I watched while Vicky was waved over to a corner of the gym by Phil and Colin. They were still whispering together as I climbed through the ropes. Hayley whistled at me and nodded towards them. She came over.

"What's going... Jesus, what's that smell?"

"My bandages," she said. "Have a sniff!"

She snapped her hands under my nose and I clouted them away.

"What are you trying to do, kill me? Why don't you wash them?"

"It's mad isn't it? How bad they smell, like. They're hummin'."

"Yeah, *nice*, anyway what're they talking about?"

"It's about Sweden," she said. "You're next... they'll call you over."

I wondered how Hayley knew who was going. She had to be guessing, I thought. I looked at Tony, sure I would read any news in his face, but I couldn't. He looked the same as always and smiled as he met my eyes.

It wasn't me next, as Hayley had predicted, but Alana. She too whispered with Phil out of earshot. Then one of the Cwmgors girls was called, and she was followed by Hayley.

There's a surprise, I thought. Everyone has been telling me a load of rubbish to get my hopes up. But I knew it was partly my own fault for getting so carried away. Somewhere though, I still felt there was a chance I'd get that red vest. I'd spent the morning sparring with the chosen four going to Sweden. I knew I had every chance for the next tour.

As the Sweden four did extra sparring, I was in tune to every muscle ache and I longed for a bath and a sit down. During my bag work Colin came over.

"You're not upright enough," he said, squaring his back and holding his hands high. I knew what he was saying. Josie's example of classic boxing and point scoring speed was very different from mine. I listened hard. I was well aware he didn't like my style of boxing.

Tony called me over once Phil had gone.

"Liz, they couldn't match you. Alana's going through, Josie too... along with Hayley and Vicky. Emma's in reserve."

I wondered whether it was my heavy-handed boxing that had kept my name off the list. Well, I reasoned, it was nothing that couldn't be changed with a little effort. At the same time, I was flat with tiredness and when Phil Jones said, "Give it a few years and perhaps you'll all be able to get your red vests!" I felt like shaking him by the shoulders and yelling, "I don't have a few years. I have to retire in a very definite two!"

That was amateur boxing law.

Back at Gelligaer, I was being watched as I observed Madoc Thomas, Ernie's grandson, in the ring. I followed his movements as the gifted teenager cornered his opponent. Madoc was another classic amateur boxer, and very successful. He'd already earned a string of wins for squad and was the proud owner of that all-important red vest.

I got a telling off for my inactivity, as I had stopped bag work to concentrate, but I called him over afterwards.

"Madoc, do me a favour... show us your stance?"

He did so, happy to help. I copied it in the mirror and then on the bags. Perhaps it would grow on me; the straight spine and elegant posture did look more polished in the mirrors. I can do this, I thought, even if it does feel a little strange.

"Lizzie!" Harry shouted. "What in God's name are you doing?"

"Keep your wig on! Colin told me to straighten my back like this... see... like Madoc does." I looked again in the mirror and admired my new style. I thought I looked great.

He shook his head, "You are what you are, Liz. You fight the way you fight and you can't change it. Squad can be great, but it can ruin fighters as well as make them. You'll go back to how you are when you're cornered and then you'll be confused; it gets messy... you forget who you are. You want to go for the jabs, sure, but go most for your shots: the short right, the hooks, the low, hard, body shots."

The other trainers were called over. They agreed.

"*Phew*," said Dai. "You catch 'em once with that short right hand of yours to the body and you won't have to hit them again!"

Tony joined in. "You don't want to start on that straight-up style. I know what Colin wants but that's not your way."

"Improve the small things they tell you but don't change your style, ok Liz?"

"Yes, but Colin... "

"Just listen will you. Squad doesn't know everything. They want everyone the same way but they're not. They're different."

"Ok Harry, I know what you're saying. Cheers!"

But I knew that Colin didn't want heart; he wanted speed. He didn't want wars; he wanted points. I hoped that Colin would be desperate enough to take a chance on a fighter and, dear God, I was going to battle for it if I got the chance. I'd make sure there was one hell of a fight.

The next day Edward phoned me out of the blue, he wanted to visit. He sat tight-kneed for warmth in my freezing flat, but he was too tactful to complain. He was subtle, but I spoke his language.

"My tea goes cold quickly... too quick to finish it. How's the flat?" he said.

"It's these storage heaters. I'll pop the kettle on again."

Edward chattered away in his soothing tone. For too long, I realised, I had lived in this frigid flat. I'd only occasionally been visited by my mum and sister with their cliquey iciness and their inability to make small talk. We didn't discuss the knockout at all. Edward filled me in on a year's worth of personal running times, sprinting techniques and the people he'd met and run with. He looked leaner in his face and shoulders. The fresh air had done him good. He was addicted to running, the harder the better. The tea cooled with exasperating speed. I wanted to hug him for all his waffle and his twittering like a canary; singing anything that came into his optimistic head. He reminded me of Julie Andrews in *The Sound of Music*.

It was as though his year's absence hadn't happened and he organised a run for the two of us. He said he could revolutionise my running, speed me up and make me even fitter. I murmured some thing about the vest. He understood straight away and he was going to help.

"It's just eight miles but I'll not lie to you. There's a bit of a hill."

It was more of a bit of a hill than I'd ever run up before. Deep breaths grew into outright wheezing for air, and still the road curled up, and up, and up. Screw the view, I thought, as my head hung. Insensible, I dragged myself up the endless road. My legs were on fire. Towards the top of the mountain, for that's how it felt, my nose dripped, eyes watered and shoulders twitched until I felt like the Hunchback of Notre Dame. I was fighting fit from squad, but this was beyond difficult.

All the way up, Edward chatted about his enthusiasm for running. Bloody show off, I thought. I hadn't been able to speak at all for five minutes and my thoughts had been reduced to a single question. How the hell could he keep it up? The hills were *alive* with the sound of Edward talking and I was half dead.

I wasn't going to let the hillsides beat me though. I loved my new routes and the view that bobbed about in front of the combs of straight, sweaty hair sticking out from my woollen hat. Time and again over the Christmas holidays I went up the slopes. I increased the distance to a ten mile run over the hills.

On the loneliest of New Year's Days I ran the ten miles yet again. I ran past old cottages and ancient, weather-nibbled gingerbread houses with their thin spirals of chimney smoke. I scared chickens who hopped onto one leg, ready to defend themselves with the other scratchy knobbled foot. Deep-eyed horses followed my path with their heavy heads and on I ran; up and down the country paths.

The landscape up there is marked by our ancestors, but it's an organic beauty: all stone and wood and soil. The earth is as darkly glutinous as Christmas pudding: every clump holding tight to its own silver sixpence. I never felt alone up there, on roads that smelt of sheep in the wet fields.

The hills were, of course, the elephants I had seen from the train that day; that first day in the valleys when I came to meet Dai. The hills wore my trainer soles smooth as I pattered back and forth across their solid shoulders; feet pecking at their skin like those tiny African birds that feast on the bugs that feast on the beasts.

On I ran, past rocky waterfalls and strange, still ponds of standing water. Birdsong drifted like confetti in the cold air. To that tune of blackbirds singing in the black-thorn bushes I welcomed in the New Year.

Despite myself I had a new optimism that day; an internal glow. I didn't recognise myself any longer but I knew that this new person would be more successful than the old. I didn't mourn the old me, although I realised that I'd lost the element of personality that, as a child, I had most wanted to keep.

The new me didn't much care.

Mum had never been much of a talker; not to me anyway. She had been busy tending to more deserving cases. However, Mum's main theme during my childhood was my heart.

"You'll have to toughen up, you know? You're heart is too big. You can't have such a big heart and love everyone and everything, because you'll end up getting hurt. Toughen up and harden up. Do you understand?"

"Why must I? Who cares if it's big? It's my heart."

"You're too soft. You're too loving. You'll have to toughen up, but you'll understand as you get older."

"No I won't."

"You'll get hurt if you don't."

No matter what age I was, it was the same conversation. I dragged my wounded way past Dad, past the bullies at school, past Sixties Steve and past Ian walking out. I prided myself on the fact that I hadn't changed; they hadn't changed me. My big marshmallow muscle of pink heart, which was all mush-mush instead of thump-thump.

As I ran down the steep slopes I wondered why I had toughened up now, but I didn't think about it too long. I was distracted by the future and the vest and prepared to work harder than ever. My new heart was as big as the old, but my mind's eye saw it as a Neolithic polished axe: worked flint, the colour of tortoiseshell and onyx, sharp as a surgeon's scalpel. With it I was going to carve a place for myself in this hard world.

CHAPTER THIRTEEN

Michael lost his excess weight overnight. His desk drawer was littered with little weighing machine printouts, through which he would monitor his progress, proud as anything; and he had started doing sit-ups and weights. I wished weight loss was as easy for me. By January, as every other girl in the office was still on Ryvita and low cal Cup-a-Soup, Michael had achieved his goal of losing two stone.

"You'll have to treat yourself! It's remarkable... so soon after Christmas. You look great."

"I am going to treat myself, well... have already treated myself. I mean apart from getting my hair done."

"Yes, I had noticed."

"Toni and Guy," he said, spiking it up with both hands. "But you are not going to believe what else."

"Okay?"

"You know Paul from Marketing? He's lost loads of weight too and, well, we were talking about losing weight and things and he said that he's been going to your old gym, Power Point."

"Yeah, he looks great too doesn't he? He was asking me only the other day where to buy boxing gloves and stuff."

"Exactly, so look at this." He pushed his keyboard back and spread the leaflet across his desk. I've signed up for this. Paul has got me and two of the boys from another department an introductory discount. Look here!"

It was a glossy leaflet promoting the Power Point Gym. Gone was the small, tatty boxing ring. In its place was a new ring, full size. They'd purchased ten more running machines and had refurbished the weights room and dance studio. There was a feature on Cleto, with a list of his boxing achievements, along with a profile of each of the fitness team. The Power Point was getting a real reputation for executive fitness. The car park filled up with even more luxury vehicles; so much so that one of the manager's friends was employed as security scarecrow to keep car thieves at bay.

Michael's first visit to the Power Point Gym was on a Friday night after work and on Monday morning I was quick to ask for details. I hadn't been there for a while and I wanted to know who'd been training him. Perhaps I knew them.

"I'm not telling you anything," he said, propping his briefcase against the wall, pulling out his fountain pen and lining it up carefully with his Counsel's notepad.

It was obvious he'd enjoyed it. He sat down and leant back in his chair a satisfied Top Cat grin on his still slightly rounded face.

"You have to tell me," I said. "What did you do? What did you make of the gym? Was Cleto there? You ought to hold the pads for him if you get the chance, it's an eye opener."

"I didn't see him. I'm not telling you anything anyway, you'll tell the girls upstairs and they'll laugh at me. I don't want them knowing I've been working on my guns. I want them to think they look like this naturally." He flexed his muscles.

I shouldn't have laughed, of course, but he was, at the end of the day, a neat, middle-class solicitor who took wine-tasting holidays in southern France.

He refused to tell me anything more, save that he was going back the following Friday and that his trainer had been impressed with his diet.

"I think it's great you're going," I said.

I looked forward to getting to the gym and telling them all about this strange new world of executive fitness clubs. I smiled to myself as I pulled into the car park.

The open gym door leaked light, but there was something else; some sense of alarm that spilled out with it. The door should have been closed to keep in the heat, but that wasn't it. I had a vague but uncomfortable feeling; a hard to define uneasiness; just *something*.

Then another indication that things weren't right; Tony darted from his car into the gym, moving too fast. A second later my dying flash of headlights caught Ernie. He stumbled out of the door, leaning his head to one side. Then he vanished in the darkness. My eyes strained to readjust. When they did, I could see Ernie pacing, pale with the anaemia of fear, as he walked in the shadows.

As I got out of the car, feeling sick, Ernie turned towards me. Clearly he didn't even know I was there. He was in shock. His hands were unsteady. He was talking on a mobile phone.

"I need an ambulance," I heard him say.

I ran into the gym.

It was one of the boys. Madoc, Ernie's grandson.

I knelt down beside him. One of the boxers whispered

to him, though he was unconscious. Tony was on Madoc's right side and the teenager was curled up as if he was home in bed, in the midst of a nightmare. He was shuddering with the tail end of a fit, his breathing shallow. His skin was bloodless, covered in a sheen of sweat.

Ernie came back into the gym. There were tears in his eyes.

"Madoc, lad, Madoc... "

He fell to his knees, scooping up his grandson's hand, squashing the limp fingers to his wet cheek.

My eyes swam with tears too.

"I never seen anything like it," Ernie said. He spoke so quiet I wasn't sure if he was talking to himself or me.

"He was on the bags and I called time. He started shaking and I thought he was messing about... to the music, like... and I said... 'Madoc what are you doing?'"

Ernie shook his head.

"Then he went stiff and collapsed. Madoc, lad... "

Ernie squeezed the little hand again.

"He's never had anything like it before Liz. He was fine. He was on the bags. He hasn't even had sparring since before Christmas. If he'd been in the ring then I wouldn't let him box again but he was fine... " Ernie's voice trailed off.

Tony tucked a couple of coats around Madoc to keep him warm. His breathing became more rhythmic and the paramedics arrived.

Madoc looked smaller covered by the overcoats. In the ring he was fit and sharp. He stood on the line between boy and man, balanced between talent and unwavering discipline. During the few times we'd sparred he was so good that I rarely caught him. I used to make a joke of it.

"If I manage to hit him once then I win a bloody goldfish!"
He was a talented, determined athlete and he was at that age where he could box with a carefree arrogance. Whatever this seizure was, it had made him a boy again.

I thought I knew enough about how life could squeeze you of your identity in a split second. I simmered about its conman cruelty; the conman cruelty of life. He was a boy; too unknowing to be cheated of his dreams and ambition in this form of medical mugging. I thought about him and his family constantly. They were terrified that Madoc might have something seriously wrong. They dreaded the thought that the gifted boy, who'd voluntarily spent seven years of his childhood in a boxing gym, might never fight again. Madoc missed his beloved squad that weekend and we all waited for the results of his scans.

Unwillingly I remembered Ian. He had never recovered from being robbed of his 'destiny', as he saw it. From the time he could march back and forth on his chubby little legs, he knew that he was an army boy. His Sergeant Major gruffness was what had attracted me to him in the first place.

Ian was made for the forces and, age fifteen, he soldiered himself straight down to the Army Careers Office. He wanted no more from life than to join a tank regiment and rumble around on gloriously muddy tracks; churning through fields and blowing things up, such as enemies and underground bunkers. He was fit, his father had been in the army and he was of above average intelligence. There was no doubt about it; he was born to wear a uniform. He merely had to get through the medical. Retelling the story almost a quarter of a century later he still despaired.

"You're fit as a fiddle young lad. I wish my son was as fit as you," the thin, overworked doctor had said with a warm smile, crackling apart the Velcro on the blood pressure equipment.

"Now for your eyes."

Ian had been reading the advisory posters on the walls. His blue eyes met the light. He could almost feel his iris growing smaller and accordingly he opened his eyes a little wider. *Nothing to hide here, Doctor.*

He then read the chart all the way to the bottom row.

"Fine, fine, no problems there," the doctor said.

The doctor took longer over the hearing test. It was an electric hearing test; the kind where you have to jam your finger in your ear. *No problem, Doctor, no problem at all.*

The doctor repeated the test and looked in his left ear.

"I'm sorry son... really sorry, but you have a hearing problem."

"What?"

"It looks serious I'm afraid."

"It can't be... how could I have a hearing problem and not know?"

"Haven't you ever noticed anything about the hearing in your left ear?"

"No, never."

"Are you sure, son?"

"No, never."

But he had. He hadn't heard the test for a start. Then half-forgotten past incidents slotted into place. Minor school work difficulties and misinterpreted conversations with friends made more sense. It was unspeakably painful. The truth was corroding destiny as solid as metal. Why did the doctor have to be so precise?

"How bad is it?"

"You are completely deaf in your left ear."

He had wanted the army and they had wanted him. They sent him to a specialist and offered to pay for any treatment that would restore his hearing. There wasn't any to be found. It tore him apart. "I should have cheated," he said. "I shouldn't have done it properly. Why didn't I cheat?"

Bitter, he had idled for a while and then turned to travelling in Europe. He worked and lived out of his rucksack on building sites, undertaking any odd jobs before returning to Wales. He was unemployed for long, dull stretches; yawning in front of daytime TV. He'd been arrested for a couple of minor offences and had frequent casual relationships which rarely lasted three months. He knew that he was behaving badly and felt justified. His deafness made him volatile and when drunk he would retaliate with violence against insulting whisperers, imagined or intended. He was aggressive and cruel when the mood took him. He was on the attack.

By the time I met him, the roaring and frothing energy was easing out a little. His anger had bubbled less hot as he found some small contentment in archaeology where he could wear fatigues, smoke pot and shout at his subordinates all at the same time. Ian stopped drinking spirits and was content to stay in during the evenings with the TV and snuggle. He was in the main affectionate and loving; some kind of cross between a hippy and a tiger. I'd never met anyone like him. I fell so in love with him that I was only a short step away from writing 'I heart Ian' on everything I owned.

I always walked on his right side.

CHAPTER FOURTEEN

The week before the January squad was a deeply unpleasant one in a way hard to explain. I was already worried about Madoc and my feeling of helpless unease was somehow echoed in the news headlines. Every paper ran a different story, but over a ten-day period it seemed they shared a common theme: girls and women being attacked.

A little girl had been abducted by a paedophile in Rumney, Cardiff and seriously hurt.

A six-year-old girl was taken from her bath and left naked in a freezing street.

Another girl from Cardiff, Katherine Horton, was abducted in Thailand as she was talking to her mother on the phone. She was raped and then her attackers left her to drown in the sea.

The sickening examples ran on and on. In the office we huddled together, read the papers and logged onto the BBC website. We cursed the nameless perverts and paedophiles.

"Sodding men should have a bloody curfew," Anna began as she closed *The Mirror* and threw it, disgusted, to my desk.

"I don't want to get on my soap box," she continued, "but they tried it in Brazil – 7pm to 7am, or something like that – for a month. It was amazing. There was no crime, no violence, nothing!"

I nodded: "It says here that ninety-five per cent of violent crime is committed by men."

"It's so scary," said Clare, shrugging helplessly.

We banded together as secretaries; rounding up our conversational caravan wagons against the unseen enemy. We were outraged. We wanted the evil attackers and paedophiles locked up. "Bring back hanging," the girls called in work, and riding home on the trains. "Bring back flogging, cut off their whatsits. That'll show them!"

"And another thing," I said. "The bloody internet is to blame. Perverts find each other, think they're all normal and treat it like some sort of goddamn club."

"You never know where they are," continued Clare seamlessly. "They look ordinary. Look at those little girls in Soham. First that bastard kills those poor children and then that investigator is done for having child pornography. They turn up all over. I mean, look at what happened to Liz!"

"Exactly," I said, jabbing the air with an arm. "Look what happened to me!"

Clare was talking about an incident some six months before, when a new tenant had moved into the flat next door to mine. He kept himself to himself, as neighbours always tell reporters later. He was colourless and nondescript. Other than seeing him leave in the morning, as we headed off to our respective workplaces, I hardly saw him at all.

A few months after he moved in, I was washing Baby when the landlord pulled up. He got out of his sleek car, his greying curls bouncing in the breeze. Usually he was distant with his businessman's concerns, but today he strode over with purpose.

"I don't mean to alarm you," he began, putting his hands up in a frank and calming manner; which made me immediately nervous.

Christ, I thought, I'm being evicted. Shit.

"I have to tell you... have a duty to tell you... the agents only told me today... I had no idea. The guy who moved in next to you, well... don't know quite how to say this but he's on probation. Seems he's a pervert. He's been sentenced to three years probation in Merthyr for attacking women. Seems he had them under surveillance and stuff. I don't want to go into details, but it was in the papers. He's lost his job of course – lab technician. Probably he won't stay if he can't find the rent money. I had to tell you because if he's any trouble... if it's a case of you or him... then he's out. You're a good tenant. If he's any bother... if he does anything... he's out!"

"What did he do?" I asked. "I should know if I'm living in the next flat to him."

"I don't want to go into it," he said again. I presumed he thought it was bad enough that I might leave there and then.

"See how you feel," he continued hastily, "and if it does get to you, I'll get him out."

I slopped the rest of the dirty carwash water into the weeds and walked into my flat more slowly than usual. I looked up at the pebble-dashed wall, my gaze stopping at my neighbour's blank window. I resented the fact that the authorities and letting agents had agreed to put him next to a woman living on her own. It had to have been arranged by someone in authority protecting him;

finding safe accommodation for him. Presumably housing him next to a single woman in a flat was ideal; nice and non-threatening for him; the kind of place where he could sleep soundly at night. It was a joke. Who was protecting me? Bloody pervert, I muttered under my breath. I grated over the times that I had held the door open for him in the mornings, and the times I'd thanked him for locking the front door after me so I didn't need to get out my keys. I bristled at every time he'd said hello on the stairs when he'd known all the while what he was.

I tried to remember what the landlord said about surveillance, and something about him being a lab technician. Ah, just forget it, I consoled myself: you're a fighter; you don't have a thing to worry about.

It goes without saying that I started looking in the obvious places where perverts might hide mini cameras and recording equipment. I'd seen stalker films. I wasn't stupid.

I checked my rickety beech bookshelf, which rocked half an inch either way, guiding it back to centre afterwards. I moved to the storage heaters with their suspicious, dusty internal grills: then the coffee table, assorted bowls and candles, the sofa, the lamps and picture frames. Next, I went through the kitchen, turning my two fish, Hamed and Barrera (Barrera being the slightly bigger of the two), into angry orange darts as I shakily examined the wall behind their tank. The kitchen appliances were inspected. I looked over the fridge freezer, slow cooker and microwave. I finished in the kitchen by accidentally knocking over the clothes horse where I hung my bandages to dry out after training.

I scouted the bedroom, but with little furniture other than the bed it didn't take long. The ideas kept coming though, and I reminded myself to save up for an actual wardrobe to replace the clothes racks. The airing cupboard was ransacked, tumbling t-shirts and towels into a dry spin. The curtains followed, then the mug tree... the vacuum cleaner... the toilet roll holder.

I listened; not quite sure for what. Something electrical perhaps; something whirring where it shouldn't be; some out-of-place signal. There was nothing other than the traffic outside on the roundabout: the usual quiet creaking of joists, the ticking of cooling storage heaters and the small human sounds of myself listening.

With increasing horror I thought about all the stuff he might've seen. There was me singing along to Dolly Parton's *Nine to Five*. There were all those yoga exercises I'd tried. Then there were the tears when I was overtired or oversensitive. There was the time I'd had a tantrum and smashed the blender. I remembered incidents of tap dancing in the kitchen (he may have heard that without surveillance). Once I'd tried limbo dancing to see how low I could go. How low could I go? *He'd seen me making myself sick.*

He hadn't seen me making myself sick because I'd checked everywhere for cameras, but he *could* have seen it. I cringed to think someone might know what a big fat mess I was in. I'd also started using Epsom salts; God help me, *even worse*. Anyone who has retched down tumblers of Epsom salts knows you have to be half crazy to drink something that tastes of copper and salt. It *never* gets any better and you *never* get used to it, as it strips your insides of anything good. I hadn't had a period for two years, amenorrhea they call it, and the books said to see a nutritionist. I thought I was getting away with it. I knew somewhere deep down in my salt-washed womb that it was out of control, but bad habits creep up on you when no one is looking.

It didn't cross my mind that watching me with an eating disorder would have put anyone off using surveillance again, even a convicted attacker. It simply brought home the fact that someone can always find you out in the end. What a strange world it was where I could temporarily be cured of the onset of full-blown bulimia by the fear of covert, pervert surveillance. That night it took me ages to drift off to sleep and before I did, I reminded myself of more places to look for cameras. Remember to check the DVDs, I told myself, and the Tupperware... and Monkey. I looked at Monkey and he stared back with glassy innocence. Check Monkey tomorrow I thought.

Screw it... if he's touched Monkey I'll bury him in the goddamn garden. Arsehole; preying on women and innocent children – and making me suspicious of my soft toys.

For a few months after my landlord's visit, I'd rarely seen him, and so I kind of forgot he was there. But I hated him for what he stood for. The guy next door, and countless bastards like him, destroyed people's lives. Life was hard enough at times as it was. It's possible, of course, that I blamed him and the world's predators for the way I felt about Madoc's situation. I had no one else to blame for it in a world that felt both dangerous and unpredictable.

Alana and I talked about Madoc on the way to squad; about how much he loved to box. We couldn't help but think of him as we faced the large number of boys across the dance studio. We stood in classic school disco line up, boys on one side, girls on the other, and waited for Phil to speak.

"We have to focus on those going to Sweden so don't feel like you're ignored if we aren't spending much time with you," he started.

I'd had a hard week, so this translated into, "*This is going to be ten different kinds of exhausting hell and we will do our utmost to ignore LIZZIE COLLINS throughout the entire thing.*"

Get a grip, I told myself.

We hopped around, kicking our feet out of our trainers, and formed a queue. I stepped on the scales. I had gone up to 64kg.

"I told you last week you've got bloody love handles," Tony said.

For God's sake, I thought, you've got to stop everyone making a joke of your weight. It had gone on for so long that it was a theme even people who didn't know me joined in on. Like all personal comments, it's fine until you're tired, or until some virtual stranger picks it up.

"Move your fat ass, *fatty*," Kathy said, as I put my trainers back on.

When it came to running it was a different matter. The hill running that Edward had put me through paid off. Josie and I, holding our places at the front of the runners, managed to chat about weight as we ran. She had the opposite issue. Colin thought she should fight at 52-54kg and she weighed 51kg.

"He thinks I can easily put weight on, but it's hard. This is my normal weight. I don't know how I'm supposed to do it, and it's not like I'm not winning at this weight. Maybe he thinks I don't eat. Of course I eat... I'm just this size."

I sympathised. Up or down, it's all hard work. I hoped that the hill running would get even more weight off, and I was pleased that keeping up with Josie was easier. I felt ten times fitter.

In the gym we were put in for sparring with some of the boys from the squad and they were fast and sharp. They cast out a lazy, casual confidence like they were playing with us. Colin leant his mouldy mahogany arms on the ropes as he watched us.

"Make 'em work but don't forget they're lesbians... ha ha, just kidding... don't forget they're girls."

"Come on now, Colin," said one of the guest trainers.

"Someone KO'd your sense of humour huh, Bob? If I had my way they wouldn't be in there at all."

The trainers talked amongst themselves.

"For crying out loud," Josie said in my ear. "Why can't he say '*Don't forget they're inexperienced*'? It's nothing to do with lesbians *or* Y bloody chromosomes."

"They need so much work..." Colin continued, half drowned out by the staccato sound of sparring, "the lot of 'em... they're out of range... too many problems... falling short... too much for them to learn... they're never going to get it... Look at 'em."

It spoiled the story Josie had told us at lunch about Finland.

"The venue was amazing," she began. "There were about twenty countries represented, but you should have seen them – especially the Americans. They had loads of stuff: matching Everlast tracksuits, beanie hats, and bags. Everything they had, matched. They're so *good*, and I mean really *good*. The sponsorship those girls get is *unreal*. There I was... the Welsh girl."

We were impressed. On the other side of the canteen

Colin frowned at us as he waited in line for the coffee pot.
"I stopped her in round two, so I can't understand why Colin wants me at 52-54kg," Josie concluded, piling her used dishes onto the canteen trolley.

"Colin told me that if the girl in Sweden does 60kg then I have to do 63kg and if she does 63kg then I have to do 60kg. Does that make sense?" Alana asked.

"I'm going to do 63kg," Kathy announced, pushing lethargic loops of watery spaghetti about on her plate.

"Surely you're too tall?"

"I'll make the weight easy. I didn't eat at all yesterday."

After the weigh-in the following morning, we had sprints in the freezing darkness outside. There was no moon and no sound except for the frenzied padding of trainers on the damp road and the ragged breathing of black shapes. Like materialising ghosts, we streamed through silver cones of lamplight dotted along the path. We raced along the road to the locked gate at the end, shaking a cold sweat of dew from the metal bars each time we rattled against them. We ran back, speeding up and slowing down as the whistles blew. When they thought we had done enough, we went to the cafeteria for breakfast, then returned to our rooms. It was gone 7.30am when the three of us gratefully moulded into the dents left in our beds from earlier. Alana fell asleep immediately, and I could hear the soft clicking of buttons on Kathy's mobile phone as I gazed out of the window.

The scene was mesmerising. The line of trees made a lattice of lead branches, splitting the china blue sky and primrose clouds into stained glass shards. A fresh breeze found its way into the room and twirled with the warmth of the radiator. I thought about weight: the endless pregnancy comments: who ate all the pies, the earthquake comments when I skipped. It wasn't that they thought I was very fat but that they believed, with all the exercise, I should be thinner. I found my weight increasingly difficult to shift.

I thought about the throwing up; the laxatives; all the weighing and worrying about every single thing I ate. As I lay on the bed, cradled in the comfort of the morning, I let go of my worries about weight. I gave it all up and let it drift through the stained glass window into the cold clouds. I had to be more sensible about it and eat properly. I had to try. I was ten stone and that was that.

I jumped off the bed and shook Alana by the feet until she sat up with a start.

"Time to get back to it."

We met up again in the dance studio where an entire wall of mirrors reflected back the sunlight coming though the opposite wall of windows, warming the still air. Kathy and I waited as the tape was rewound, so that it could screech out its timed bleeps again. She readjusted her gold hair clips as we sat down on our purple foam exercise mats.

A small part of the sit-up bleep test had been tricky for me ever since I broke my elbow. Although my arm no longer hurt when I threw a jab, I still couldn't do the plank exercise well because you have to hold your weight on your elbows and forearms. I'd kept it a secret, and thankfully no one had paid that much attention to my elbow, but one of the pins jutted out under the skin. It wasn't a problem, except that I couldn't lean on it too well. If I leant on it in the wrong way it felt like being stabbed with a knife. When the bleeps came and they shouted 'plank' I had to twist my arm awkwardly to avoid the lumpy scar. As I held the position I thought about Kathy. I'd been thinking how different we were, and that she was crazy for getting her nose broken and carrying on almost immediately, but hadn't I done the same thing with my arm? I wanted to ask her why she was so determined but I couldn't. What if she had said it was because her old man thought she was a waste of space? What would that say about us? I could imagine some crazy psychologist stroking his goatee and saying, "yes, of course, *dahling*, they are simply angry at their fathers". You can think too much in this game.

Kathy interrupted my wanderings as we got up off the mats and waited for the sparring.

"Phil Jones had a chat with me last night," she said. "He's got about four other tours coming up, one to Ireland... one to Hungary. I'm not sure where the others are. But anyway, I'll be going and he said I'll be doing 66kg to 69kg."

She said she ate a big salad at lunch to account for this and I got on better than ever with her at squad. But I realised, later, that I had never seen her eat anything at all.

On Monday night I stayed out of Harry's way in the gym. I was very fond of the professional trainer who relayed endless stories about his exploits with Dai and George when they had been training Cleto. However, amongst his many jokes was a running theme on my weight, and I was trying to take my mind off it. I had to face him in the end, but he was distracted and I remembered that he had recently adopted another, more controversial, focus.

I joined him on the low bench by the mirrors where he was in mid-rant. He pushed his glasses up the bridge of his nose in a scholarly fashion; someone who knows a thing or two.

"I'm gonna burn it down as soon as it opens and the first person as gets attacked by someone from that place, I'll put a brick through the counsellor's window!"

"I saw the posters in the back of your car," I said.

"Aye, and I'll keep putting them up as well. Bloody drug misuse centre right in the middle of bloody Tir Y Berth and all them church people say it's a good idea like but, aye... and I'll tell you this, there'll be druggies and alcoholics and paedos. I don't mean to scare you Lizzie, right, but you live on your own... and imagine you're getting home after dark and finding a pervert living on your doorstep. Would you feel safe? *Would you?* Be honest, Lizzie... can you think of anything *worse*?"

Sure, being fat and living next to a pervert. That was worse.

I noticed Ernie keeping time; his back warming against the heater.

"Any news from the scans?" I asked.

"They found something but they haven't said what. He'll go back in February. The doctor says they're treating it as epilepsy. What if it happens again? It's terrible."

If it turned out to be epilepsy then he'd lead a normal life but they'd never let him box again.

"How're his mum and dad?" I enquired.

The tough man in front of me sagged, and his eyes filled.

"I'm sorry... they went through something similar when he was born. His lung collapsed. It was touch and go. That's why they called him Madoc, he's a little fighter see." He shrugged, helpless.

"You're going to start me off now. And Madoc, how's he holding up?"

"I told him today; he came round after school and talked about it after in the car. He cried his eyes out... broke his heart... "

"Bloody hell, Ern, I'm sorry. I'll be thinking of you all until he has the next scan... really I will."

"I'm hoping that it'll be clear and then I can tell him it was a false alarm. It hasn't even hit him yet. Even when he was in the hospital he was saying, 'I'll be ok for squad though won't I?' He lives for squad... lives for boxing."

It was something Ernie couldn't fix with his spanner.

When I got home I savagely poked up two fingers at my next-door-neighbour's window.

CHAPTER FIFTEEN

I was on the train to work when I got a text from Michael. It read "I won't be in – MH". I closed my phone and thought nothing of it. Must be ill, I assumed, reading my horoscope. The woman next to me shifted as my paper brushed against her arm, so I folded it shut and slipped it into my carrier bag. It joined my lunch, along with two bits of past-best fruit. It was a shame my companion couldn't do the same with her pithy perfume, a mix of citrus with heavy notes of spray tan.

I made the most of Michael's absence by sorting his post and then ate my dripping conference pear at my desk. Had Michael been in, I would have been listening to his considered opinion on something vitally important, such as whether the Bond girl for January was better than the Bond girl for March. He had already removed February (Grace Jones) with a pair of scissors and sent her soaring in a compact ball into the bin.

"Look," he said, beaming at his ingenuity. "I've got Ursula Andress two months in a row! Everyone's a winner."

Except Grace Jones.

It was a peaceful and productive day. I had time to catch up with the weekend events of my colleagues and still type a good pile of letters. Michael will be pleased, I thought.

By the afternoon I began to wonder where he was; how he was. People were asking if he'd taken the day off to go somewhere, whether he was ill. He had looked fine on Friday. It had to be a personal problem; his mum probably. She'd had a hip replacement – all sorts of complications apparently.

Suddenly, Ruby, who sat at the desk opposite mine and talked so loud that I often had to turn my dictaphone up, raced in breathless. She was balancing the scarlet cup carrier loaded with tea and coffee, which streamed down the side of the plastic cups.

"Oh my God... Oh my *God*, you'll never believe what's happened and you are in *big* trouble. *I can't believe it.*" Ruby brushed aside her glossy black fringe which fanned across her eyes.

The *you are in big trouble* bit had been directed at me with a nod of her head. She handed round the cups with a "sorry, sorry everyone," as each secretary wiped away the running coffee and tea rings with a hand or paper towel. The girls wheeled back their chairs into the centre of the room and looked at Ruby and me.

"It's terrible," Ruby continued. Whatever it was though, she looked amused so it couldn't be that bad. "I didn't know that Michael had been training at Lizzie's old gym."

"Oh yes," said Chloe. "It's all part of his new man, midlife-crisis thing that he's going through, the funky facial hair; the trendy clothes; the diet. What's happened?"

"Well, I was down in the kitchen and Paul from marketing was there, right? He said, 'Have you heard about Michael? Does Lizzie know?' And I said, 'Does

Lizzie know what?' And he said, 'About what happened to Michael at Power Point on Friday,' and I said 'No, she hasn't said anything,' and he said, 'Well, some guy broke Michael's jaw'."

The secretaries exploded en masse; a star burst of exclamations and excited horror.

I was speechless. He'd only been going to the Power Point Gym for four weeks. I phoned Paul and got the story, as far as he knew it. Then I called Michael and spoke to his wife. I was so sorry that I was beside myself, and I was fuming, absolutely fuming at the idiot responsible.

Michael had turned up for training on the Friday night, but was told his trainer was running half an hour late. He decided he might as well warm up on some of the equipment. Curious, he picked up a pair of bag gloves and threw a few punches on the heavy bag.

"You might have made a good boxer, you know," said a man behind him. "There's a bit of power in those shots. If you'd had proper training you might've been alright."

Michael had been flattered and entertained. The guy looked like he'd boxed.

"Have you been in the ring?" Michael asked.

"I can handle myself," he replied, moving his shoulders. "I'm Richard," he said.

"Michael," he said, throwing another punch at the bag.

"Have you ever done any boxing?"

Michael put his hand on the ring ropes. "No," he said, "never tried."

"Check out this ring, it's brand new, must have cost a fortune. I was here when they set it up. Tell you what, get those bigger gloves on and I'll teach you a couple of things. You never know when you might need it."

The first round had been, of course, totally one sided.

Michael's confidence had increased. From time to time the guy would remove his blocking elbows to allow Michael the experience of landing shots.

By the second round Michael was exhausted and sucking for air. The routine changed, perhaps to allow Michael to get his breath back. Richard said he was going to throw one or two back, but not full, maybe fifty per cent of his power. They shuffled round the ring and hardly a shot was thrown. Richard then decided to offer Michael some advice and stopped in front of him. As Richard started to speak, Michael, misreading the open defence, punched him square in the face. Richard instinctively replied with a stiff and professional uppercut which almost propelled Michael out of the ring.

Michael lost consciousness for about five minutes and when he came to they eased him through the ropes and sat him on the side of the ring. The trainer who had been booked to train Michael turned up at the same moment as Michael was being half-carried to Richard's car. He was driven to the Accident and Emergency Unit at the Heath Hospital in Cardiff. Michael's wife was angry that Richard didn't take him straight to Caerphilly Miners' Hospital, but neither of them knew where it was.

Michael was well aware that he'd broken his jaw because the pain was killing him and he could barely speak. He sat there dazed, unable to open his mouth and he was mortified to realise that at least two of his teeth were loose.

"You total tit head," he mumbled shakily at Richard.

He had refused to talk to Richard after that. It hurt too much, his teeth wobbled when he spoke and Michael didn't care if he took it personally. He worried about how he looked, thinking of the Elephant Man, and about what his wife and children were going to think. He murmured to Richard, who was looking confused as to how it all happened, asking him to phone his wife and tell her to come to the hospital.

When the doctor examined him, Michael was introduced to new levels of agony. He found trying to open his mouth excrutiating. Any more than about a centimetre wide and the pain became unbearable. He felt like his lower jaw might fall off altogether and clatter around the doctor's feet.

"Just a little bit wider... I know it hurts."

"Ah cahn't, *argh*."

"That's enough. Time to get you X-rayed but I don't think they'll tell us much more than we already know. You have a fracture of the lower mandible and two of your teeth are going to have to come out." The X-rays confirmed as much. "We will have to keep you in. Follow the blue arrows. You'll see the sign for the Maxillofacial Department. They'll see you at reception there."

Michael was still in the waiting room forty-five minutes later when his wife arrived. Richard patted him gently on the shoulder and explained everything that had happened, before apologising and departing.

My boss had promptly been admitted to a ward and the following morning had, under general anaesthetic, an operation to put his jaw back in its correct position. Whilst there, they also removed the two lose teeth. He was discharged on the Sunday and his youngest daughter burst into tears when seeing her father, not because he looked much different, but because Daddy looked so sad.

When Michael made it back to the Power Point to collect his car, it had been stolen.

He didn't return to work at all that week. Nor did he phone in.

I had to tell Edward.

Edward Creed's favourite pastime was running, but he gained a secondary warm sense of pleasure from gossip. He was the sort of gentle type who could entertain old ladies for hours with a small amount of gossip and a large slice of Victoria sponge. He would adore the drama of this, and it would do him good to feel that he wasn't the only one who'd had a tough time in the ring. When I sent the email to his office I swear I could hear him lapping at the words in the same way his mother's poodle went at the leftover steak. The reply was in upper case, using streams of exclamation marks and contained something very unusual for Edward. He asked for his very first favour.

Not long after Edward's knockout, social services had stepped in to help him care for his aged and housebound mother. He'd been doing his best, but was struggling to hold down a full-time job and care for her in a house so dilapidated that the central heating had been tripping the electricity. At any one time there seemed to be either heat or light, never both. There was an inquiry as to how a pensioner could have been allowed to live in such conditions and a grant was given for basic home improvements. The British Legion had been called in, as Edward's father had served in the army, and they sent over a builder to take notes. The list was surprising to say the least, starting with panes of glass for Edward's bedroom window. He hadn't had the time or money to fix it himself. Hot water plumbing was recommended for the kitchen, as was a washing machine. He'd been washing everything by hand.

As builders and carpenters came, scratched their heads and left, Edward was inspired. Eventually he decided to go the whole way and decorate, with a view to selling the property. His request was that I spend Saturday afternoon stripping wallpaper in his house, and at the same time I could fill him in on the events which put Michael in hospital. The ensuing eighteen lines of the email dripped with a humble succession of "please don't feel that you have tos" and "just say if you're busys," with more of the eternal exclamation marks. I thought of him sat in his office with his fingers jammed on shift and 1 until he felt the necessary spaces were filled in.

Of course I would go round there. He'd helped me learn to drive, helped me move, and had been my running and fitness partner. It was the least I could do. I read the first three lines of his lengthy and grateful reply to my acceptance and pressed delete.

Edward hired a wallpaper steamer to make things easier. He steamed, I scraped, and we filled the room with the smell of hot paper and cold plaster. It was a satisfying afternoon making that paper scroll off in long, winding curls. Our conversation about Michael rolled off as easily.

The walls behind the paper were mottled cinnamon, and I loved the way the colours warmed the room. He had already done a good deal and after a few hours it was finished. Then we tried to mow up the old green carpet lengthways with a Stanley knife. It seemed a good idea to slice it and roll it up like turf, but it was hard going. Edward paused to chat about our old boxing training and the Power Point Gym for long stretches and, sat neatly on his heels, his progress slowed.

"We've made great headway," he said, wiping the carpet fluff from his reddened hands. "I've bought lining paper for the walls and I should have it done by next weekend."

It was a shame because he was intending to paint the room white. I wanted him to be more adventurous but it seemed he saved his colour palette for his gym wear.

When Michael returned to work the following week he was withdrawn and miserable. He was restricted to a soft diet. He couldn't open his mouth properly. He had trouble sleeping. His jaw clicked every time he tried to open it and it made him feel sick. I checked on him all the time.

"How are you feeling?" I asked.

"Guess where I've been," he said with care.

"Where? You were gone a while."

"I was over in the Personal Injury Department, and they say I have a case. Hell, I say that I have a case. The legal guidelines give about £6,000 compensation for a case like mine." He rubbed his jaw, gingerly opening and closing his mouth.

"Let's see what this guy has to say to that. He phoned me the other day, you know. To ask how I was doing, which is something, I suppose. He said it was a freak accident. *Freak accident*, he's having a laugh... the guy punched me."

I reminded him that boxing is a tough sport, and these things happen. I also told him about Edward and it seemed to make him feel better.

"But you sparred with Cleto Basiletti didn't you?" Michael asked. "You didn't get hurt?"

"That's the point. They teach you how to avoid being hurt. It's a skill, something you can't pick up from a couple of minutes in a ring. It takes years of practice."

"But he still must punch hard."

"I've never known anyone punch harder than Cleto, it's like being hit with a hammer."

"So how...? I mean... you must have amazing defence."

"Of course I've learned to defend myself, and then there's the other thing."

"Which is?"

"I have a head like a coconut."

I smiled and went to leave.

"Just one more thing... " he said, hesitating. "Richard said on the phone that it had only been fifty per cent of his power."

"Like hell it was."

"Are you sure?" he said, his voice loaded with need.

"Of course I am... one hundred per cent sure."

It was on the second Sunday in February that Edward arranged his 'thank you, Liz' dinner, thrown in aid of the paltry couple of hours gossiping and scraping the previous weekend. There's no need I told him, typed him, texted him. Since it was only the second thing he had ever asked me to do, I only had so much room to refuse.

He showed me around his current DIY efforts and thanked me for coming over.

"Papering only took me four days. Around the windows was fiddly but I'm not going to live here that long so I didn't worry about getting it perfect. You can see where I cut around the light switches. Not too brilliant is it? But it's alright."

It did look alright, I agreed, yet it remained a Spartan geography of self-conscious furniture. Apart from the thirty-six inch TV, which dominated the lower end of the room, there was only a bony sofa, covered with an orange throw, and a small stick table and two chairs; the hard kind with banister rail backs and legs.

"I'll brighten it up with some more furniture when I have the time," he said. "So, you must be ready for something to eat."

"Sure am, something smells lovely."

"It's pin bone steak from my favourite butchers. Cost a fortune but I like it just right. Sixteen pounds for the two, but worth it I think."

I tried to keep from thinking about his mum sat in her bedroom, his years with the Welsh weather blowing straight in through his bedroom window, and the lack of hot water.

"I've got some nice veg and home-made bread. And just in case you're worried about germs I made it with gloves on."

"Edward, I don't mean to be funny but you're too weird, you know? I can't imagine why you'd think I was the kind of person who'd have bread made only by people wearing gloves."

"I bought them in Kitchens, the catering shop, just in case."

"Let's not talk about gloves anymore, Ed."

He brought the plates to the table and carefully placed down the food.

"It looks great, but I can't possibly eat any of it unless you made it wearing a hair net."

"You're making fun of me now."

"Stop being so strange then."

It was a nice enough meal but he fussed too much. He always was a bit off the wall but he kept on at me. Did I like the food? Was the meat alright? Did I want some music? And so on and so forth. It wasn't conversation so much as me constantly having to reassure him that everything was perfect. I tried to drag the table talk back to Michael's injury.

"So, Edward, I can't believe... "

"I'm just going to the toilet a sec... "

"Are you alright? You don't look well."

He was sweating yet the room was chill. Something was very wrong. Whatever it was I didn't like it. The meal was getting weirder but I couldn't think of a reasonable excuse for going early that wouldn't hurt his feelings.

He came back in looking liverish and lost in thought as he walked to the table.

"Edward, I'm feeling a little uncomfortable, I should... "

"One minute," he said.

Edward let his small, bird-like hand settle on the back of his chair and went to sit down but he missed.

He missed... and dropped to one knee.

"I've come to realise that if I'm going to spend the rest of my life with someone then I want it to be with someone like you," he said.

Edward opened a small, navy leather box, in which sat his mother's diamond ring. I knew it was his mother's even without being told and I was choked. Edward looked at me with an expression somewhere between apology and hope.

I wanted to scram all the wallpaper off with my nails; the way a cornered cat would. I can't remember all the excuses I gave him. There was something about being too busy to get involved, and something about not ruining friendship, and something about me still not being quite over Ian.

It's an awful thing, but it annoyed the hell out of me that he took it so well; like in the old days when he used to thank me for punching him hard. Then it was as if we ran out of words. It wasn't an uncomfortable silence but a thoughtful, digestive one where I reviewed our whole friendship in seconds and concluded that I was a complete moron. I should have spotted the signs. I should have noticed. I thought further and further back. Stupid, stupid, I thought... it sort of all made sense, the moving, the driving... and *the sparring*. I remembered his first reluctant time in the ring and last bit of sparring with me at Gelligaer. Cleto's instruction to go easy on him came back to me and I realised that Cleto had had an idea how the guy felt.

I didn't want to think about it anymore. I wanted to go home.

"What made you do it?" I asked, rising to leave as he smoothed the outside of the ring box as if comforting it against the rejection.

"I think we get on well," he began. "And after I hadn't seen you for ages and then we started talking again, I thought perhaps you missed me so you might... you might... you know... and then it was this weekend and it seemed appropriate."

"What weekend?"

"February the twelfth."

"Huh?" I was sure his birthday was later in the year.

"Valentine's Day!"

"I think that's usually on the fourteenth."

"I knew you wouldn't come round if it was the fourteenth."

"Right."

CHAPTER SIXTEEN

It's not my fault, I thought. Edward hadn't given me a clue. I remembered that in the first month of training us, Cleto had hinted from time to time that Edward was going to ask me out. He had also mentioned that he thought Edward was acting like a 'bit of a wuss'. Disbelieving, I watched Edward for a while anyway, in case. There had been nothing. I had never seen so much as a twinkle in his eye.

I was concerned about to how to deal with it in work. Monday morning, being February 13, brought out the annual big Valentine debate. Speculation was rife as to who would receive the ostentatious bouquet of burgundy roses. There's always one monumental spray delivered to a secretary with a card that reads something along the lines of "To Jean, with love. Terry." We all translate it into "*To Jean, I'm assuming this size bouquet is showy enough to make all the other secretaries wish they were going out with me as well – and I'm expecting sex, Terry.*" It makes us feel better.

For the girls, learning I'd received an offer of marriage would be real office gossip. It would be with salted humour that I'd have to endure the endless questions, the laughter and the resurrection of the subject every time the name Edward came up in any conversation. Of course it was funny in a way, but it was sad too. I wanted to laugh it off and forget about it in my own time. I resolved to keep quiet and see how things went.

I opened my various folders on the computer, and was hit with a wave of nausea as an email showed up from Edward. No, I thought as I considered it, please leave me alone, but I knew I had to open it. That innocent little banana yellow envelope perched at the bottom of my screen, inviting me to slip on it and fall on my face. I clicked twice on it and it was so long I had to print it off for an easier read.

Dear Lizzie,

I know that you probably hate me and I'm the last person you want to hear from but please, please let me explain myself.

Ever since we met I felt like you needed me because your husband had gone and you didn't have anything or anyone and you were starting all over again, so I felt like you needed a guardian angel and I thought I could watch over you, especially when you said about boxing. I thought if ever there was a lost soul who needed a guardian angel it was you.

That's why I trained at the Power Point so often because I wanted to make sure nothing untoward happened to you. (That's not to say I didn't enjoy training with you because I did!!!) See, my motives were totally honourable, which is funny really because I found it much tougher than you did. I was upset that I couldn't go up to Gelligaer. That's why I wanted that guy to teach me. I thought maybe if I was a bit better, Cleto would let me box there too.

But anyway I thought that you would learn your lesson at some point and I would be there to help you. I know that I never said as much but I don't really think girls should box. Not that you're not good or anything but just that it's too tough a sport, just look what happened to me!!!

That's why it was my pleasure to help you learn to drive and help with your move and that time I brought you up that huge, massive Persil from Macro so you didn't have to buy those heavy boxes when you went shopping and those mega, massive tins of plum tomatoes and those bars of Dove soap.

I have always hidden my feelings from you as I thought that I was better off being your guardian angel and not complicating things, but then you seemed to be getting on your feet. I thought then, when we met up again, that perhaps you had missed me, just like I missed you and perhaps you realised that I was your guardian angel after all.

I'm aware in this day and age that people rush into relationships and live together but I consider myself to be more gentlemanly than that. I am not one to force my religion down other people's throats but my mother and I are committed Christians and so I wanted to do things properly. (I would not have expected you to become a Christian by the way!!!)

I'm sorry I've messed things up. I really am sorry and if there is any way you can forgive me, then please find it in your heart because I only ever had honourable intentions to look after you!!! I will understand if you never want to speak to me again and I can only say that I'm sorry.

Yours, Edward x

Well, that explains it, I thought, having read it twice. He thought I was a lost soul who needed looking after. No guardian angel of mine would have been knocked out. It was unthinkable. I emailed him back simply, "It's all forgotten," but I had every intention of keeping a good distance. The point of those twenty-four Dove soap bars sitting under my sink was going to have to remain eternally ambiguous.

I was reading Edward's email through again when Michael phoned. Please leave me alone, I thought, for the second time that morning. I told him that I was on my way to his room.

"Guess who was on the phone," he said.

"Who?"

"The *South Wales Echo*! I don't know how they got hold of the story but they know about my injury. They said there's been a few like it around the country, now that boxing training is getting more popular."

"What did you tell them?"

"Told them what happened. There's no point pretending it didn't. It might stop someone else doing the same thing."

"Are they going to interview you?"

"Yes, I'm not sure if it'll be in the papers tonight... it might be though. They're sending a journalist round here at eleven thirty. Will you say anything to them? You know about this sort of thing."

"No, I'd rather keep out of it."

"Thought you might."

I felt drained and sick. My glands were swollen and I wondered if I was coming down with something. I wouldn't have minded. A couple of days spent hiding under the duvet sounded idyllic.

The journalist turned up on the dot and I showed her

up to Michael's room. She was much younger than I thought she'd be. She looked like one of those girls you see on Saturday morning television – milk-teeth smile, doll-pink cheeks and ruthless ambition. She said that the photographer was running five minutes late but she might as well start now. After introducing her to Michael and closing the panelled door on them, I sighed. She was probably ten years younger than me but already had an authority to her voice which said she was going places, she was going all the way to the top... and she was happy to peer into the world of boxing on the way.

The light wasn't right in Michael's room so they used the conference room for the photographs and I watched from the door as he looked the right degree of downright mournful.

"It'll be in tomorrow's edition," the reporter said to Michael, "as long as I can speak to a doctor today about boxing injuries. If not, then it will be the day after.

She smiled him her *Breakfast News* smile.

"Will you need to speak to me again?" Michael asked, trying to look as if his interest was a professional enquiry.

"Possibly... but I've got a good deal here."

They shook hands and her heels clicked from the office at speed. The photographer tried to keep up and attach the Velcro to his lens bags at the same time.

Michael flapped his hands at me to get me back up the stairs; reminding me I had work to do.

"What a babe!" he said.

"You'd never keep up with her," I replied, thinking of the poor photographer.

The article was published in the *South Wales Echo* the next day and in the *Western Mail* the day after.

LOUISE WALSH

Boxing Training – Fitness on the Back Foot?

The use of boxing techniques for fitness training has been steadily increasing in popularity, but is there a darker side to the phenomenon? Take the incident that occurred at Caerphilly's recently renovated Power Point Gym. Michael Harrington, a solicitor with Cardiff-based Don Rankin and Marshall Solicitors ended up in hospital with a broken jaw and missing two back teeth after an unsupervised sparring session with another gym user, an incident which mirrors the brutality of the 1999 film, *Fight Club*.

"I just wanted to get fit, and maybe download a bit of stress, but this has added to my problems, and I had to take a week off work to recover from my injury," said Michael, from Thornhill, Cardiff.

Peter Deans, the manager of the Power Point Gym, said: "Every possible precaution is taken to ensure the safety of our clients. Safety within the Power Point Gym is really paramount. What happened to Michael is an unfortunate, but isolated, incident and I wish him well in his recovery."

Valerie Sharples, spokeswoman for the British Medical Association, has called for a complete ban on boxing. "Boxing is not a sport that can be made safe," she said. "Even the use of the training methods in community gyms is frowned upon by the BMA. No other sport holds injuring an opponent as its core aim as boxing does. Michael Harrington's case shows that serious injuries are still common."

She added: "If you are punched to the head there will be brain damage on some level."

I was reluctant to go to the gym as I was tired of discussing events with everyone – Edward, Michael, the girls in work, the guys at the gym. I was fortunate that evening as it was quiet, with only Ernie watching over the amateurs, and Tony and Dai keeping an eye on the professionals. It was better than I'd hoped as none of them had seen the papers and I launched into my training appreciating the lack of debate. I asked Ernie again about Madoc's results. They had yet another scan to go, although it looked more positive.

"You know how it is," he said. "Because it's boxing they need six doctors to agree rather than just the one."

I left early that evening. As a result of having so much on my mind, and having been proposed to by Edward only two nights before, I hadn't had a chance to go shopping. Furthermore, I loved food shopping. I could spend hours in a supermarket looking at food, window shopping the fancy cakes and chocolates, but only buying the same not very exciting things – mostly brown rice, skimmed milk and apples.

I didn't get home until after 8pm. Groaning, I heaved my ASDA bags up the stairs. The landing bulb had blown days before and I only remembered it every time I got back in the dark and had to fumble about in the shadows. I was getting annoyed at having to scrape the key blindly in the general direction of the lock until it clicked home. The forty-watt bulb that lit the dingy entrance hall couldn't penetrate the gloom on the top landing, but six nights in a row I had forgotten to call the landlord.

By the time I got to my flat door, the keys were cutting into my hands along with the thin threads of the carrier handles. I was happy to put the shopping bags down. They sagged and spread at my feet, and their plastic crackled to my sigh of relief. The crackle was immediately followed by the scratch of keys in my next door neighbour's lock. His door opened, flooding light into the hallway. Silhouetted, he looked as though he had forgotten to brush his hair.

"You look loaded down," he said. "Need a hand?"

"No, ta, I've got it," I said, faking such brightness it might have lit the light bulb.

"Bulb's blown," he said. "I would have called the landlord but I've lost his number. Don't suppose you've got it?"

"Yeah, but I don't mind giving him a call in the morning."

I held open my door with a foot and began to scoop up all the shopping bags.

"Let me give you a hand."

I started to tell him I was fine but, before I could finish, he picked up three bags and took them into my flat. I wasn't sure what to do. I was hardly in a position to be rude. He found his way into the kitchen and took a good look round.

"This is a massive kitchen compared with mine," he said. "I've always wanted to check out this flat. You know, I like to see what other people are getting for their money. Would you mind giving me the landlord's number though? I might need it for something else... in case something else goes wrong."

"Sure."

I found the number in my phone and wrote it down for him on a scrap of paper.

"Thanks," he said. "I'll let you get on."

He saw himself out. I heard the door click closed behind him. I stood there for a moment, relieved he had gone. I continued unpacking the shopping. It occurred to me how funny it was that he had said he'd always wanted to check out my flat – him being a surveillance pest. That was something to make the girls in work laugh. I put the milk in the fridge but as I did so an awful thought occurred to me. I hadn't heard or seen anything to make me think it... and yet... I paused. I tried not to panic. I stood up and turned to find him leaning casually in the doorway.

I couldn't say a thing.

"When it comes down to it – you're all the same, aren't you," he said.

"Sorry?"

He was blocking the doorway.

"Using people, yep? You never even said thanks."

Hadn't I thanked him? I couldn't remember.

My cheeks burnt with embarrassment; the humiliation of being told off by a stranger. I thanked him, sounding hollow and insincere. His face twisted. He leaned against the wall, seemingly quite at home in my home, and folded his arms. I stood stiffly, like a visitor.

There was no way past him.

"Hey, but, look, don't take any notice of me. I'm just having one of those days," he continued. "Forget about it. We could be civilised; friends."

I thought of calling for help, but nothing had happened. I knew I would sound crazy. He smiled, as he continued to lounge against the door frame looking around the kitchen. He spotted the clothes horse and I could see his curiosity piqued.

"What's that all about?"

He meant the bandages. There were eight of them stretched on the clothes horse after I'd rinsed them in the bath the night before. They were perfectly dry and hung there like rags. They'd been used and rinsed, used and rinsed until they'd turned grey from sweat, floor exercises and from traces of mascara when I wiped my eyes. Three of them still held a faint but obvious residue of blood from my scarred knuckles, a repeat pattern of brownish yellow patches.

"It's nothing... " I replied. "Look, I have to get on... really, I need you to leave."

"Have you been hurt? Is that what they're for?" he asked. He sighed, and reached out a sympathetic hand. I shrugged away from him.

"Hey," he said, insulted. I tried to dart around him but he stood right in my way. I recognised his deodorant – Physio-Sport. My legs began to shake.

"Hey," I echoed, looking to get around him as he threatened to cut me off whichever direction I went in. "Get out."

A memory stirred from years before. Big Jim was talking defence; a get-out clause against a drunk in a bar. *"Okay, so someone is getting aggressive. For example, you are up against someone who's had too much to drink. If you can't get out of it by walking away then do this. Put your hands up like you surrender. That's the way, the way they do it in the movies. Then you say 'Can I buy you a pint?'... Then, before they answer, you punch them as hard as you can."*

I put up both my hands.

"I'm sorry," I began, "I don't know what you... "

His hand flashed back, as if preparing to strike me, but then he crumpled to the floor as if his feet had vanished from under him. It was a punch so fast it surprised both of us. My right hand hit him in the stomach with every pound of my bodyweight riding in behind it. I cupped my burning fist with my left hand, ready to hit him again... or run. Where would I run to?

He curled up, swearing.

"Please," I said. "Get out."

"I've had stomach surgery you stupid bitch. I wasn't

174

going to touch you. For fuck's sake... " He smacked the lino as if the agony was unbearable.

I didn't know what to do. I couldn't phone the police. It was my word against his. They'd arrest me. I grabbed his foot and started to drag him out of the flat.

"Don't... don't," he pleaded. "What the hell are you doing?"

I didn't know what I was doing.

He didn't try to put up a fight until I got him to the top of the stairs. Then, throwing me a look of pained repulsion, he gave in and even sort of assisted me in getting him down them.

"I need an ambulance. I'm hurt. I'm gonna fucking do you for assault."

As I neared the front door I noticed his t-shirt had ridden up from friction against the dirty, buff carpet. I could see an angry vertical scar, jagged red, slightly reflective and almost papery thin with its newness. I was stunned, although I tried to show no reaction. He'd been telling the truth. I'd assumed he had been lying. It seemed weird that predators like him would have normal, human things like operations.

I wasn't sorry for punching him because it had just happened – I hadn't really planned it. I was sorry for hitting him there though. I was silent as I dragged him out into the freezing street. I slammed the front door.

Once I'd locked myself in, I found my mobile phone. Squeezing it tight, I slid down onto the floor and stayed there. I sat in semi darkness. I had a good view of my flat door, but hoped I couldn't be seen if someone looked through the keyhole. There wasn't enough air. I don't know how long I sat there, listening. I sat until I felt bits of me going numb. I listened to people walking past the flats. I heard two blokes talking loudly to each other in the street, one breaking into a howling laugh and the other swearing jovially. I watched the car headlights as their white beams swung though the vertical blinds and swept across the living room walls like searchlights in a stand of trees. I sat there trying to remember exactly what had happened in case the police came. I wondered if he would come back.

After a long while I heard a siren, distant but getting louder. I got up and hobbled to the living room window overlooking the roundabout. I held my breath. It was only an ambulance heading for Blackwood. I went into the bedroom and sat on the bed, cuddling Monkey. I was too shocked even to cry.

He moved out that week while I was in work. It all seemed like an intense nightmare in daylight. I was scared going out and coming back to the flat. I told no one. The guys at the gym would have wanted to kill him, and they would have also been angry that I hadn't told them that I was living next to a convicted attacker.

The girls in the office were content with a perfunctory "The pervert's gone." They merely replied with a "Thank God for that, I bet you're pleased." I was too.

I phoned the landlord and he put in a new light bulb.

CHAPTER SEVENTEEN

I was edgy in the weeks that followed the incident in my kitchen. I expected him to be hiding in my flat when I got home. I checked every room before going in, like I was Cagney or Lacey. I thought he would come back. The car park behind the flats felt lonelier and set further back from the road than usual. The unlit steps up to street level looked steeper and way more dangerous.

It felt safe in the gym, so I was even less inclined to leave than usual. I sat there biding my time, watching the trainers huddled, open-mouthed, over *The Echo* like carol singers over a song sheet.

"*Phewee*," Dai whistled. "Cleto wants to get out of that Power Point set up. He's too good for them. I've told him, he's got to come back and work with me."

They were even discussing it at squad. Everyone was wondering why people often think boxing is just a matter of putting on a pair of gloves and trying to beat someone to death.

Everyone shook their heads.

I enjoyed squad more every time I went there. Slowly I fitted in. The girls were friendly and funny, and I found myself spending less and less time on my own. I was tempted by games of football, gossip and listening to music. I'd never experienced that sort of rough friendship before and was delighted to discover that it wasn't that I couldn't fit in, but that I had been inexperienced and shy of company.

We raced, we hurdled, sparred and skipped, and on Sunday Phil Jones made his stolid way over and pulled me aside. His brown eyes scrutinised me.

"I don't know that you'll be good enough. You're fit, but are you up to it? That's what I'm wondering."

"Good enough for what?"

"For Norway."

They were taking three girls along. Alana and Hayley were also picked. Phil instructed us that we were off to Norway in five weeks time and that he would contact our trainers with all the necessary information. I couldn't concentrate after that. I went through the exercise tests but I was no longer there, I was already in Norway.

I sat in my parents' living room not looking at my dad. I rarely spent any time in the same room as my father. In the first house we lived in my dad had a separate living room. Although anti-social, it at least allowed his family to relax in the other rooms. The living room in this house was open; fine if he was in a people-tolerant mood, which he rarely was. I examined my nails as I weighed things up. The trip to Norway was something to be proud of. Under normal circumstances I would tell my mum any news I had, and she would tell my dad when I was half-way down the street. I couldn't decide whether to be brave about it and tell both of them at the same time.

Dad was watching UK Gold. Jeremy Brett was camping up his Sherlock Holmes and it was the episode where the lady finds an ear in a box of salt. He'd probably seen it forty times. Then all of a sudden the statement popped out of my mouth as if it knew I was distracted by Holmes, seen its chance to escape and bolted like a common criminal.

"Guess what," I said.

"What?" Mum asked.

"I'm going to box in Norway with the squad."

"What?" Dad barked, with one eye on Mrs Hudson and Sherlock.

"I'm going to box in Norway with the squad."

"I boxed Norway," he said. He coughed, and shifted in his chair.

"You boxed in Norway?"

"No, I boxed Norway, *over here.*"

"Oh."

I was surprised by his sudden admission. I was ignorant of his experiences in boxing.

"How did it go? When you boxed Nor... "

"I used to polish your grandfather's trophies. I don't suppose you would remember them. They were on the sideboard for years. Your nan didn't mind as long as she didn't have to polish them herself. I kept the boxing quiet and she wasn't amused when she found out I was going to Central Boys Club."

"She didn't like you boxing?"

"It wasn't that. They didn't care what you did as long as it was Catholic and Central Boys wasn't Catholic. It wasn't even a real boxing gym anyway. They just had some amateur trainers. I ended up for a bit at England's Gym where the pro fighters trained, but then they said you couldn't spar the professionals when you were amateur so I went back to Central."

I didn't know if he had finished or not. He paused to

drink his tea and light a cigarette. I looked around the room. It had its usual empty hollowness. My mum didn't like ornaments or pictures so, apart from the furniture, there was only a carriage clock on the mantelpiece and a couple of prints of ships in harbour hung in the two alcoves. There wasn't much else. I couldn't even see a newspaper to pick up and I was still trying not to look at my dad. I was relieved that there was at least a window and three sparrows flitting backwards and forwards in the box hedge.

Dad ground out his cigarette and continued talking. The sparrows took off.

"They pulled me out of school early, even though they knew I loved going there. All the teachers knew I was good at art and literature but you couldn't argue with your nan and grampy. I had to work for my father on the buildings, sweeping up, carrying stuff. Barry, my mate, persuaded me to go to Central Boys after work, to get it out of my system. He said at least some of my old school mates hung round there so I could still see them all.

"The thing was – I was knackered. I wasn't used to working like that and I was trying to work out a way of still going to school, so I wasn't as sharp as I should have been. The trainers at the gym said to spar with Barry. We clashed heads and he cut my eyebrow open – blood everywhere. Your nan knew all about it then. Every now and again I popped in to catch up with the boys but I lost heart after that. The scar was in danger of opening up all the time. Just a couple of extra years and I could've finished my education and started on the buildings then. You don't know how bloody lucky you are – with the constant, sodding rubbish you come out with!"

The *Sherlock Holmes* volume rose by five on-screen

dots like bullet holes from the barrel of his final sentence. I thought it had been going rather well up until then.

Mum and I sat in the kitchen afterwards.

"Can you believe it?" she said, wiping over the pristine hob with a damp J cloth. "He hasn't talked that much in ages. I'm always trying to get him to talk to me but he'll turn up the TV or read the papers. All the magazines I read say, 'try to encourage your partner to open up,' but I never get anywhere. Some days I know full well he's read the *Echo* twice over, but he still won't speak."

Everyone in our family knew that Dad had been taken out of school to work on the buildings, and that he'd felt cheated ever since. However, it was strange to hear him admit that he'd lost heart and I thought it was sad that he'd lost it so early on.

CHAPTER EIGHTEEN

Ian had gone into archaeology for one reason only, and that was his love of anything Viking. He'd claimed some sort of tenuous Viking ancestry from the first, but I dismissed it as pretension; the same way that Sixties Steve had an East London accent having visited the city once. Ian admired the Viking spirit, their designs and their exploration. He had long, book-bowed shelves of glossy Viking histories and files upon files of dusty academic papers relating to the same. On the walls he had A5 clip frames containing all kinds of pen and ink illustrations of Viking pins, sewing needles and other household basics. I used to think the Vikings would have thought it strange had they seen him carefully framing a drawing of one of their carved hair combs. Considering that I was the one who left archaeology, it felt very odd that it was I, and not Ian, who stepped first onto Norwegian turf.

Cardiff Airport was quiet at 6am so I found it easy to spot the three trainers, Ronnie, Dave and Phil, who were keeping a close watch on the two boys who were also fighting.

It was my first time on a plane. As a kid I had watched

those white planes, like slices of chalk scratching the sky; filled with travellers on great journeys. It was a lot to take in when I think about it: flying, fighting abroad for the first time and representing Wales. I wanted to feel the weight of making a small contribution to women's boxing history. I hoped to feel a sense of destiny in being able to claim the red vest as my own. I expected to feel a little more significant as a person. I didn't though. The last thing I had been prepared for was to be reminded at every turn of Ian and his obsession with the Viking history of Norway.

I was supposed to be all focussed on boxing.

I loved the little bit of Norway I saw, travelling the short journey from Oslo to Tønsberg but, too soon, we reached the hotel. It was a clean and modern place. The inside was a welcoming mixture of soft lighting, sage walls and carpets the colour of clear honey. After dropping off our bags we were asked to weigh in and then we headed for the hotel restaurant.

"This is minging," Alana said to Hayley, over the platters of plastic-looking, processed meat.

"We're going to starve."

I helped myself to a salad roll.

Hayley and Alana decided to get food outside the hotel and I trailed after them. The town struck me as both beautiful and strange. It was pretty, in an old-fashioned sort of way. If it had been in sepia it would have looked a picturesque, Norwegian answer to the wood-panelled shops you saw in photographs of the old Wild West. We ambled along Tønsberg Brygge's streets as the temperature dropped to the point where the empty tables and chairs outside a café just weren't inviting, despite the bright canvas awnings.

"Where's the bloody McDonald's?" Hayley asked Alana.

I had been content with looking in shop windows, but it was getting bitterly cold so I turned back for the warmth of the hotel, leaving Hayley and Alana to continue their search for burgers.

Back at the hotel, the quarter-final sheets had gone up, listing who was fighting who the following morning. Male and female boxers crossed backwards and forwards to the papers. I ran my finger down the list. I was drawn against a girl from Sweden. Alana was drawn against a girl from Ireland, and Hayley would take on a Finn.

The three of us spent the evening wondering what tomorrow had in store.

"Do you know the tall boy who's with us?" Alana asked. "Ronnie was saying he's picked against an Egyptian ranked third in the world."

"Not that massive bloke?" said Hayley.

I knew who she meant and he was the biggest, most unfit-looking Egyptian you ever saw.

"No, stupid, the other Egyptian. Third in the world. That's the luck of the draw isn't it?"

None of us slept well. We were all up far too early, looking grey and confused with tiredness. The tea was terrible.

The boxing didn't start until 11am and I was on first. I could feel the nerves in my stomach and it felt like I'd eaten a selection of dumbbells. I'd been thinking for too long. All morning there had been little else to do. I tried hard to think about 'the positives'. I told myself over and over that I had got the red vest. It didn't seem real though. If it was supposed to make me happy – it didn't.

I didn't feel much like a winner. I wasn't sure I deserved the red vest in the first place. I felt the other way, as if I'd lost something.

Phil Jones pulled it out of the plastic and handed it to me.

"But Phil, it's blue."

"That's right. Didn't you see the list? You're in the blue corner."

"A blue red vest?"

I held the cobalt-blue top in my hands. It had the usual Welsh embroidery but it was blue. Nothing ever turns out like you expect. I got changed and walked into the Conference Hall with Ronnie and Phil. They celebrated amateur boxing properly in Norway. There were disco lights pulsing and Puff Daddy's *Come with Me* blaring from the speakers.

"Oh yeah," said Ronnie, "I forgot to tell you about that. They put a little more in over here."

"I'll say."

Back home, ring entrances to music are banned in amateur boxing.

I climbed through the ropes and looked at my opponent, who swayed in her corner from side to side to loosen up. She stopped moving about and stared back at me with grey, challenging eyes. The music died and we were announced.

I met her at the centre of the ring and we touched gloves.

"Defend yourselves at all times," the referee said.

The bell went.

She was good. Singly, her punches weren't hard but they were cumulative in both points and power. My inexperience in big competitions was obvious. She was way in front and when I accidentally caught her round the back of the head I stuck out my glove to apologise. She ignored it. It was a club show habit and she had no intention of being friendly. It didn't make a difference to the fight other than as another example of how out of my depth I was. She displayed an enviable amount of ringcraft and her lead soon became unassailable. Before the end of round two she had done enough. It was over. It had felt like seconds and had lasted only a matter of minutes. I escaped with little damage other than bleeding knuckles where the barely healed scars from squad had rubbed open afresh. I didn't get much sympathy.

"I *told* you to piss on them!" Alana said.

Alana's fight wasn't much different from mine. Her opponent was the European Champ. Hayley, however, won confidently enough to showboat in round two, and she made it through to the semi finals on the Saturday. We were overjoyed. She had been our last hope for a medal for the girls.

We watched the young men boxing. As the lumbering Egyptian heaved himself into the ring for a quarter final against a heavyweight from Scotland, we knew it would be a good fight. The three of us couldn't help a snigger because the Egyptian was really bordering on obese. He turned out to have a real flair for footwork though. As his Scottish opponent raced at him across the ring, the mighty but swift Egyptian nipped aside and the Scotsman fell out of the ring, like a tossed caber.

We rocked with laughter. Before Alana went to sleep that evening she laughed again about it.

"That Egyptian... he was so fat though!"

Hayley boxed again the next day and, hands cupping her face in a peek-a-boo guard, she narrowly out-pointed her rival. She was setting a great example. We wondered whether she would go all the way. It was almost too much to hope for. Later her opponent failed to show up for the final. No reason was given. She asked Phil what it meant.

"What does it mean?" he said. "It means a walkover. It means you've got gold."

She would have preferred to get it by boxing but it was a gold medal for Wales and that was what counted. We spent all afternoon watching the finals and in the early evening we attended the award ceremony to watch Hayley and spot the other girls to look out for in the future. The Irish had triumphed overall. I had expected the Norwegians to run away with the medals, as we were on their turf, but the Irish had fought off everyone.

That evening we were all invited out on the town by two bruised Norwegian girls who had both suffered, quite literally, at the hands of the Irish. I declined, feeling flat. I fancied a bit of time to myself to have a bath, relax for a while, and sort out my belongings which were tangled up in my holdall. I also wanted to plan a little sightseeing for the following day as we weren't leaving until the evening. I'd ask at reception if they could recommend anywhere to go.

I must have been fast asleep when the girls came back. I awoke early the next morning having slept undisturbed. I tidied my bed, kicked Hayley's bandages to the far side of the room, and headed down to breakfast.

Neither of them had moved when I returned and, as Hayley mumbled in her sleep and turned over, I left a note on my bed saying that if I wasn't downstairs in the hotel then I was having a wander around town and would be back later.

As soon as I was clear of the hotel I gave a delighted shiver of relief. I was free: the lone tourist. I headed down towards Tønsberg Brygge and the harbour. The Norwegian Sunday was quiet as a convent, lacking only a church-bell peal. A strong morning sun lit the slatted wooden homes to chilled champagne. A stiff breeze dried my mouth. I licked my lips in the wind and felt the sharp nicks the gum guard had caused. My neck ached a little. I took a big breath in and it felt like I was sheltered in the calm of the lagoon. It was so still I wondered if you would get bored of it eventually, or whether you'd slip into an early-retirement lifestyle. Perhaps you'd take up gentle hobbies like negotiating a sailboat around the islets, or gardening. I gave it some thought and concluded that I would never get tired of it. I might come back again, I thought, for a holiday, if I ever had any money.

A chill crosswind got behind my back and pushed me sideways and forwards towards the front. It was deserted apart from a solitary figure a short walk away, sat facing the sea. I strolled towards her.

The woman was sat on a bench wrapped in the thickest jumper ever made. Her silver Celtic-knot earrings rested flat on the wide, polo-neck knit collar. She wore a bun in her white-grey hair and escaped threads of hair pulled in different directions like silver kite strings. She had to have been there a while because her nose and ears were crimson.

"It's beautiful," I said, looking at the pen and ink sketch she was working on of two little boats in the harbour.

"That's where the beauty is," she said, pointing at the boats which nodded their noses in gentle agreement. They lay on the sapphire water with clean, white-windowed tops and hulls of light, varnished wood, full of dark knots like ink stains and signatures on the flap faces of old school desks.

Her name was Mary and she was an artist from Uxbridge. Her husband, Teddy, was a photographer who had first visited Norway six years before when they fell in love with the place. He came for the scenery as he was a landscape and wildlife photographer. When they could, they holidayed in Norway in all the different seasons.

"There isn't anywhere like Norway," she said.

"I'm leaving this evening so I'll have to come back another year. There's not enough time."

"Look, don't feel like you have to, but Teddy and I are off to Verdens Ende in half an hour. We'll only be a couple of hours at most. Would you like to join us? It's only a half-hour drive and you can't leave until you've seen Verdens Ende. Do you know what it means?"

"Haven't a clue," I said.

"It means 'World's End'. If you are going to come all this way you may as well see it through to the end." She smiled. "We'll be going soon. If you want to come along, and you are not doing anything else, you'll be more than welcome."

It felt risky, but the cynic in me said the most damaging people were the ones I saw every day. These people – they were just being kind.

"I will... if you're sure you don't mind."

Chatting, we walked back to her hotel, The Golden Tulip.

Teddy warmly shook my hand before I got in their hire car and Mary filled him in on the boxing and my visit to Tønsberg. He was old-time handsome with his silver-fox hair and trimmed white beard. Teddy had heard of the Norway Box Cup before but admitted to having little interest in sport other than the occasional game of golf.

"Have you tried the delights of salted cod yet?"

I laughed. "Yes, I had a sort of tomato and fish stew thing. They didn't tell us it was salted cod. I was one of the few to finish it. I don't eat much salt. We all thought it had been made with sea water but you have to persevere don't you?"

Teddy settled into driving and humming Elvis songs under his breath; Mary pointed out landmarks, picturesque buildings and chapels.

As we drove down the south road we passed lagoons and creeks, like the setting of an Enid Blyton adventure. I wanted to stop the car and explore. I longed to run up to the pastel, kit-model holiday cabins and peer in at their windows to see what their furniture looked like. I imagined Shaker styles: goat-skin rugs and patchwork quilts; plain wooden tables set with bread and pale cheeses but I was probably wrong.

The sound of the seawater pressed against the shore washed over us as we got out of the car. I looked at my watch. It had only taken thirty-five minutes. I took a quick look at the lighthouse but wandered down to the first jetty. I ran my hands along the silky bleached wood of the handrail, and it creaked lightly.

'World's End,' I thought, and it was like the end of something. Ian would have loved this place, but he had left me. I felt I had come a long way since then, and it was time to forget him. My thoughts drifted to the Vikings and their long ships, imagining them sailing off, cutting and slicing through the dark blue glass, and somehow, quite without meaning to, I imagined Ian in one of those boats. He was that type of person, you know; the kind who wanted to move on and explore. He was the sort of man you couldn't pin down for long and while he had said goodbye to me a long time ago, I hadn't been ready then to say it back. I missed him too much.

I said goodbye to him across the sea because I didn't know where he was. I hoped the sea wind might take it to him and I wished him well. *Bye Boo.*

Walking back across the rickety jetty, trainers tapping the kippered wood, I made my way over to Mary. Teddy was further on, clicking his camera, taking his pictures of the sea and the slumped boulders on the water's edge. I wondered if the two of them had ever said goodbye only to recognise it as a mistake.

"Aren't you doing any sketches?" I asked Mary.

"I've just finished a couple but we're here for Ted really. He won't be long." Ted started to pack up his lenses.

Mary struggled up the rock Teddy stood on. She found it steep and wobbled as the wind wrenched at her long skirt. Teddy reached out a hand, pulled her up and spun her round, bending her back in a waltz finale.

"You two look like you're dancing on the back of a whale," I said.

They looked down at the pale grey rocks, like dolphins and whales carved in stone. The one they stood on was particularly like a large sea-mammal. Teddy smiled.

"You think outside the box don't you," he said. "Mary, I think Lizzie here may be an artist on the quiet!"

"Sure, martial artist," I joked, but I was flattered.

We headed back. I realised how tired the fresh air had made me. In the car Mary smoothed back her straying hair and chatted to Teddy about home and their neighbour, who was looking after the house and who might have forgotten to feed Fizzy the cat. Mary started to sort through the sketches on her lap and Teddy hummed Elvis songs to himself again.

"This one's for you," she said, turning awkwardly in her seat.

"I can't... it was good of you letting me come to Verdens Ende in the first place!"

"It's yours... a souvenir."

I took the sketch from her. It was an ink drawing of me on the jetty looking out to sea.

"It's beautiful. I'll have to get a decent frame for it."

"What were you thinking about out there?"

"Salted cod," I said.

Teddy chuckled and nodded in agreement, "I've given it much thought myself!" he said. And he hummed the opening bars of *Heartbreak Hotel*.

CHAPTER NINETEEN

When I got back to my flat on Monday, it was late afternoon. Although I had lost, fighting in Norway had brought changes. I was filled with a content and a sleepy feeling that probably came from a sense of relief. I felt sort of buoyant – as light as the scudding, cloud-clipped sunshine that had followed me from Norway. The adventure abroad had made me miss home, and I couldn't wait to sink back into my routine and habit.

I steamed away in a bubble bath, eyes half open, listening to Donovan's *Sunshine Superman* album. I mulled over my home. Rented bathrooms are all the same. I suppose landlords are awarded a free supply of sloppily grouted, grey, green or buff marble-effect tiles every time they redecorate a bathroom. In this bathroom they were buff marbled tiles and lino. I found it oddly depressing. Every time I had a bath I would think of how many times I had steamed up the same cheap tiles in different colours. Not quite as many as I've had hot dinners but then that was another depressing count in itself – how many hot dinners were ending up in the bathroom.

One day, to cheer myself up, I bought one of those

sunny miniature rosebushes sprinkled with tiny yellow buds, and I put it on the bathroom window sill. But over the following months I spent more time leaning over the toilet, looking at the wallpaper shadows cast by the rose leaves on the lino than I did admiring the plant itself.

The two fingers I wanted to stick up at the world I stuck down my throat instead; stuck them up to me and my health.

I knew the girls in the office would filter out most of the information and remember only the fact that I didn't make it through to the semi finals. I gave them a quick report and settled down to work. I knew I would get a better reception from the trainers that evening. I looked forward to seeing them all again.

The evening came at last. I swung Baby into the gym car park and pulled up in front of a black Lexus. Well, I thought, someone's got some money. It dawned on me then, the personalised number plate read F1 GHT. Cleto must have bought a new car. I wondered what he was doing in there. I dawdled past the ebony gloss of his motor and paused outside the gym. On tip toe, I peeked through a small triangle of clear glass at the corner of a poster-obliterated window. I couldn't see him. After swinging open the door I stopped in surprise.

"Wow," I said.

Tony was inside the door squatting by the kettle.

"Tell me about it," he replied.

Madoc held the centre of the boxing ring, keeping off his friend and opponent with a flash of gloves, and over in the corner Cleto was taking little Ben on the pads.

"How long have I been away, Tony?" I asked.

"Isn't it great about Madoc?" he drawled. His eyes

looked watery, but it could have been his cigarette smoke. He looked away and filled his mug, placing it carefully on the chocolate-brown plastic chair to cool.

"I thought that was it for him," he said. "Ernie thinks that the hospital doctors were being over-cautious because he'd said Madoc was an amateur boxer. They couldn't find anything. In the end a load of them agreed that there was nothing to stop him getting back to it."

"Yeah, and he's looking even sharper."

"The break's done him good. He's always trained hard. He probably needed the rest anyway." Tony's roll-your-own snapped up and down as he spoke and I realised it was stuck to the left side of his bottom lip with his dried spit. Older people never drink enough water. I caught Ernie's eye and he gave a lopsided grin and directed his gaze to Cleto with an almost imperceptible nod of his head.

I threw him a look of amused surprise.

"I didn't expect to see Cleto, Tone."

"Neither did we. I'll tell you after he's gone. Anyway, I spoke to Alana's mother. You all did well over there."

"I tried, but it was some experience I can tell you."

I talked to Tony and Ernie about Norway while I skipped, and now and again Ernie would lean with his shoulder towards Cleto; his eyes filled with mischief. They were obviously pleased to have their champ back. I couldn't wait until Cleto got out of the gym and Tony had the chance to explain.

Wrapping my hands I glanced over at Cleto as little Ben jumped up at the pads held a fraction too high for the small boy. Cleto wore a duck-egg blue rugby top, so tight that his torso was a series of hills and dips as he moved. I marvelled that he was still only a fraction less conditioned than he was at the peak of his career. How old was he now, thirty-seven, thirty-eight perhaps? Behind Cleto was a large poster advertising an old fight of his in Poland, with him squaring up to a Roman-nosed opponent. Cleto nodded at me as I began jabbing at a bag. I waved back.

I did three rounds on the bags as Cleto gave another boy a workout. When they next called time Cleto jumped in the ring.

"Come on, Lizzie," he instructed, gesturing with a pad still on his hand. "You used to like this."

"Thanks Cleto," I said, as I ducked through the ropes. I never tired of pad work. It was like a game, hitting the targets as they popped up – like play. Nevertheless, I'd forgotten how exhausting it was on the pads with him. The red circles popped up fast. By the time the first round was over I leant forward, my gloved hands curling around my knees, trying to catch my breath.

"I'm sorry to hear about your boss," Cleto said. "How's he doing?"

"Accidents happen. He's fine now, pretty much. I think he might have been put off boxing forever though."

"Such an awful thing. It should never have happened."

"I know."

The round started again and he held up the pads. I settled into his relentless pace and started letting my shots go; enjoying myself.

"She's a banger," said a new boxer watching at the side of the ring.

"Oh aye, she can't half punch," Harry replied. "She's recently come back from Norway, boxing for Wales."

Another three minutes was punched through and the round came to an end.

"Anyway," Cleto said, "I've finished with the gym in Caerphilly for now. Maybe I'll open my own boxing gym, but Dai asked if I'd help him out for a bit, help out with the boys and things."

"You'll be up here more then?"

Dai was going to be overjoyed. I looked around for him but couldn't spot him. I laughed as the boxer next to Harry winked at me. *Cheek!*

They called for the boxers to start again.

"One more round, Liz? Yeah, I'll probably be up three times a week."

Afterwards, as I climbed through the ropes, having thanked Cleto, he stopped me one last time.

"You still hear from Edward?"

"No, not anymore."

"He fancied you, you know."

"Mm, yeah," I said.

"If only he'd have been a bit more up front about it," Cleto said.

It wouldn't have made any difference to the unromantic outcome, but I had to admit that it was sort of true, from Edward's point of view at least.

An hour later, Cleto shook Dai's hand and then drove off in his Lexus, throwing up a cloud of car-park gravel behind his tyres. I asked Tony what was going on as we sat down with a cup of tea. He explained Cleto had left the Power Point Gym for good. Dai had always encouraged him to return. They all agreed it was the best way, until Cleto decided what he wanted to do long term.

"There was only one thing that stood in Cleto's way," said Tony.

"What was that?"

"Me, Babes, it's my gym too remember, not just

Dai's. This is an amateur and professional boxing gym. Fifty fifty."

"What happened then?"

"Let's just say that I've ordered an enormous frickin' sack full of new stuff for our amateurs, from an anonymous donor." He waved his thumb at a picture of Cleto.

"He didn't?"

"Oh aye, very generous too. Can't complain. Didn't George always say you'd get your money's worth up here?"

We sat together grinning.

"Here's to George," he said, raising his tea, and our mugs clinked. "And how's your car doing?"

"Don't spoil it, Tone," I said.

CHAPTER TWENTY

I raced for the gym door chased by some hugely obese storm clouds, a sky full of Sumo wrestlers all barging and shoving and gearing up for one hell of a fight. The air hummed with electricity.

"Have you seen it out there?" I said.

They agreed it was turning into a monster.

I said hello to everyone and was stopped by Cleto as I walked past him. He'd been turning up at the gym three times a week and had begun to show a growing interest in my activities at squad.

I smiled back at him as he beamed at me.

"I hear congratulations are in order," he said, looking as if he'd caught me out; as if he had uncovered a secret of mine that I should have shared.

"What for?" I asked, turning over every squad tour possibility.

"You're engaged aren't you?"

"Not that I'm aware of," I laughed, thinking he'd lost his mind.

"Harry said that you were engaged and getting married on May the eleventh."

"I guess I'll have to speak to Harry."

I spotted Harry cleaning his glasses, standing in his Gore-Tex coat, over by the mirrors. He was reading a list of professional boxing rankings that had been stuck up in a corner. I hooked him in the ribs twice, gently of course, then started skipping next to him.

"What's this about you marrying me off?"

"Hello Liz. Aye, the wedding. It made sense, see, I fancied some wedding cake and it's about time some lucky guy made a decent woman of you. Anyway, someone's been asking about you, and I could really *do* with a nice bit of cake, an end bit, you know, with lots of icing in that shape they make." Harry made a scallop shape in the air with a finger.

"Who's been asking about me? Are you pulling my leg because if it's cake you're after then I can sort you out without having to go to the bother of marrying someone. My sister makes them."

"No, dead serious now. He saw you on the pads with Cleto the other week. His name's Alex. He used to come in years ago when he was a kid and he's turned up again to get fit, like. He was asking all about you. I told him not to bother 'cos you talk funny being as you're from Cardiff and your nose is getting squashed through all the boxing."

"Cheers Harry, as long as you put him straight," I said.

"See, I didn't understand a word you said just then. Why don't you try writing it down for God's sake."

He did his usual gag of repeating what I said whilst squashing his nose flat. "*Jeers Yarry, 'slong as you pud 'im sraighd.*"

"Why May the eleventh?" I asked.

"Thought it would be a good date."

Thank God he hadn't picked May 19, I thought. It

would have been too weird.

Thunder crashed overhead. We looked up, as if one of those Sumos might come straight through the ceiling. Stiletto rain followed after, stamping down like the heels of an angry crowd.

"Well then, the weather will need to be better than this," I warned, coiling my rope and putting the wraps and gloves on.

"So is it true?" Madoc called over from behind a bag. "Congratulations."

I told Fay about the wedding story as we rode the train into work the next morning. The storm had passed over and left a blue and breezy sky, rinsed squeaky clean. Fay was wrestling her newspaper into her bulging mock-croc bag.

"What's this Alex like then?" she asked, as the paper jumped out of the bag and landed on the feet of the bored conductor, who rolled his eyes without smiling.

Fay apologised as we showed him the tickets. I waited for the newspaper fracas to end, feeling like she had missed the point. It was supposed to be a funny story. Finally, she wedged the paper in the jaws of the croc and sat up as if ready.

"I dunno what he's like really, Fay. I hardly saw him. He was probably thinking that I punch hard, that's all. Anyway, you know I'm too busy for all that, but what's Harry like, eh? Telling everyone I'm getting married!"

"Liz, now be honest, how many dates have you been on since Ian?"

"I'm busy," I said, a little defensive. "You know full well I can't fit in any other commitments. I'd have to sacrifice something and I've sacrificed all I'm going to for men.

Any sacrifices now, I make for me."

"Promise me you'll think about it if he asks you out or something."

"You've got it all wrong. Firstly, there's no way he's going to ask me out. You should see the state of me when I'm training. Secondly, I'm way too busy with work and everything. I couldn't find the time!"

"Just promise me you'll think about it."

"I don't know why you're so keen, but I promise." I knew full well he'd never ask anyway.

We chatted around the subject, talking of work and how the mornings were getting lighter, but towards Cardiff, rumbling along at the back of the student accommodation blocks, she seemed a little sorry.

"It's only that I care," she said. "You deserve better, and sometimes I think you don't do yourself any favours."

"How do you mean?" I said.

"Well, you seem to have only a few ways of dealing with men, you'll fight for or against them, and if you can't do either then you don't seem to see them at all."

I thought about it in silence for a second, looking out of the train window. Some of those students still had tinsel Christmas decorations up.

"Perhaps you're right," I said. "But, you know, I reckon it goes further than that even. I think you may have just summed me up. You know something else though? Sometimes, I think the only reason people don't fight is because someone else does the fighting for them. No one else ever fights for me, Fay, you know?"

"Just think about it, Liz. You need to lighten up a bit," she said, and she smiled that smile of hers where her eyes told of a tired courage, shaded with sadness.

Michael complained that morning that I should get my hand sorted out because it looked awful. It didn't look that bad, but after I bumped my weeping knuckles for the third time, pulling cumbersome files out of his cabinet, I agreed. At lunch I trotted to Boots the Chemist and found the hydrocolloid plasters in the first-aid section. I paid and made my way out, reading the back of the packet. I bumped into a man on his way into the shop. I apologised and then laughed.

"Edward, fancy seeing you... I'm really sorry, I wasn't looking where I was going. How are you doing?"

He looked like he was going to spontaneously combust with joy.

"Sema," he said, "come here. This is the girl I was telling you about – the boxer. This is my friend Lizzie."

He pulled Sema towards him and introduced us. She was a tiny girl, compared with me anyway. They had come from a visit to the museum, their second visit in a month because Sema couldn't get enough of it. She held Edward's arm, peeking out from behind a thick dark brown fringe and trying to smile whilst biting her lip. She had heard all about the boxing and seemed like a nice, shy girl, but I was going to be late for work if I stayed any longer. Edward promised to phone me that evening.

"I'm so lucky!" Edward began when he called. "What did you think of her?"

I sat on the bedroom window sill, looking down the valley as the ravens rose and fell; their calls sounding like the creaking of wet wood about to break.

"She's lovely Edward. How did you meet?"

"It's a funny story really. I'm friendly with my butcher in Cardiff Market and he has this friend who's from

Israel and he knew a couple of Turkish friends and other nationalities. Anyway, he said he knew of this girl who was working as an au pair in Cardiff, but she was very shy and didn't go anywhere. He thought I'd be the perfect person to take her around as I'm so friendly. The family she was with didn't take her anywhere. I suppose they were too busy, so the only place she went once was Alton Towers. The guy she works for is a chemist or something and writes books – text books, I think.

"We've been everywhere this month. Sema loves universities and museums – so we've done Oxford and Cambridge, and the museums in London. She's fascinated. Women don't get much of a chance at that sort of thing in Turkey she says. She keeps saying that when she has children they'll go to university whether they're boys or girls. I said to her, 'Don't force it down them or you'll put them off the idea.' I know it's quick but I proposed. We get on really well, Liz. I'm going over to Turkey in July to meet her family. That's going to be scary. She said her father expects her to marry from the same village. I'm sorry I didn't tell you right away but I wanted to make sure Sema felt the same way as me, and I didn't know whether to... you know, what with the... you know."

"That's daft," I replied. "I'm overjoyed for you both. You deserve a bit of happiness. Only, when's the wedding?"

"We haven't set a date yet but sometime next year. Maybe, maybe you'd like to be a bridesmaid... I mean, don't worry about it if not... you know, you might not like that sort of... "

"Count me in Edward, I love weddings. If you like I'll ask sis to do the cake."

"Oh, that's great, brilliant, wonderful, fantastic, well

done, superb... "

I was delighted for him and it gave me hope. At least one of us knew what they were doing.

In the weeks after Norway I was unsettled. I suppose it was an anticlimax. I felt I was waiting for something else to happen. I'd planned, as soon as I had the vest, to get an identical picture to the one of Gramps. However, since the vest wasn't red, and I hadn't won the fight, I didn't want the photograph. I hadn't earned it, and in not having the photograph taken I'd lost my way. I couldn't see where I was going next.

I was thinking of all this on a morning run, whilst listening to my MP3. I was almost home when a bolt of pain shot through my stomach. I jerked forward, bent double, needing the bathroom. It was agony and I knew that the salts had caused it. The pain subsided, leaving a cold grease of sweat on my upper lip and forehead. The running was over. The fastest I could go was a wobbly speed-walk. A car rolled past. I stood up as straight and walked as normally as I could manage. My hands shook as I tugged the headphones out of my ears. The pain burst up again, rolling like the thunder of an unexpected summer storm after the first flash of lightning. I arched again and hurried on, clutching my waist. I hurled myself through the flat door, flinging the keys to the carpet as tides of pain came in sharp spasms.

I chucked the salts away, but found the damage I'd done to my stomach remained for some time. It was a harsh lesson, but I knew that truly I had escaped lightly. It occurred to me that it could easily happen again on a squad run if I didn't sort myself out. The thought of that alone started my stomach churning. I heeded the warning and I'd purged myself for the last time.

Suddenly, I was sorry for having treated myself so shabbily. I realised with surprise that I wanted to make it up to myself. In trying to get those knives out of my back, I'd stupidly gone and added a couple of my own.

I had a spell of gentle swimming instead, whilst my over-sensitive stomach recovered. There were some good pools around and my favourite was Cefn Fforest, an ancient box of lazy waves, which I leaned through in a thoughtful crawl. No wonder I had taken to swimming I thought, shaking the water from my leaking goggles, it was close to what I was doing in the rest of my life; treading water.

I had returned from a Saturday afternoon swim when Tony called me up.

"Phil Jones called," he said. "Are you free from the twentieth to the twenty-third of April? That's Thursday to Sunday."

"I could get the time off. Why? What's happening?"

"I've been asking 'em for years and they've finally said yes. It's the first frickin' Women's Four Nations Championships. It's at the same time as the Schoolboy's Four Nations Tournament in Dublin. Madoc's boxing over there as well. I'll be going too. You've got a match. Just get the frickin' time off for Chrissakes!"

"Wait a minute Tony, you're not pulling my leg are you?"

"Dead serious Liz, I've been asking them for ages."

"You better be, today's April the first."

"Huh?"

"April fool's."

"Christ, course it is. I'll have to phone Harry and tell

him you've been arrested for tomming. That's a good one."

"He'll be gutted! He's looking forward to my wedding."

Tony laughed and hung up. I snapped the mobile shut.
Ireland.

CHAPTER TWENTY-ONE

In Norway the tatters of my marriage had trailed behind me like a ripped wedding veil, snagging on things and snapping me to attention at unlikely moments. So now I anticipated thinking about Grampy when I went to Ireland. After all, I was the one he had stood up in the middle of the garish carpet to dance with him. I would perform a clumsy, self-conscious hop to the Memorex cassette warbling out Irish jigs. As I danced, he would clap his rheumatic hands in delight. But as it turned out I wasn't distracted by the past and the trip, other than in boxing terms, felt empty. This time, it seemed, it was about the fight.

The coach picked us up in the ASDA car park at 10.30pm. Colin Pickle was already on board; his chin drooping onto his chest fuzz. Tony dropped down next to him. Madoc slouched against the window and whispered to his grandfather. It was going to be a long night of stops and starts, more pick-ups at various services; one in Swansea. Josie and I sat together.

"Have you been to Dublin before?" she asked.

"Nope, don't know much about it other than that it's where my nan's family came from. Oh, and if I remember rightly, it was founded by the Vikings in eight hundred and something or other." *Them again.*

We chatted on for a while until the rising moon lengthened the shadows on our words. We softened to a hush and then stopped.

We met the ferry at Fishguard at 2.45am. By the time we reached Dublin we were in a dull dream, rolling through the hotel corridor to our rooms. Our heads felt gorged with tiredness when they finally plopped onto our pillows. The moment for a good sleep had gone; over-ripe and bruised.

We woke late on Thursday. Josie and I wandered through a mash of visitors feeling hung-over with fatigue. It was only after a lunch, though not much of it, that I started to revive and brighten, even though I was still shy of eating in public.

I fell in love with the shopping areas, and the handsome musicians pulling jigs and airs from any bit of varnished wood with holes or wires. I had to be dragged from the entrance to Penneys by an impatient Josie. I'm sure she wished she was there alone.

Josie and I showed up at the National Stadium for the weigh-in and medical at 7pm. There were fewer girls than I'd expected. I recognised two of the English girls, and one Irish boxer from photos I had seen in Ernie's *Boxing News* clippings. Their fame made them more forbidding.

Colin explained that, as there were so few girls, I would box in the final, there being only one girl available in my weight. Essentially this meant that I would get an automatic silver or gold depending on the result. I was delighted at this. Noting that my Irish opponent was the European champion, I was going to have to earn the medal anyway. Josie would have to box in the semi-finals at 2pm the next day.

Before her fight, Josie joined me for a coffee in the Ringside Club. She'd fought the girl from Scotland once before and had won the fight, so she was hoping for a repeat.

At 1.30pm we had a parade. The Four Nations were represented by their flags held by a nominated boxer in the four corners of the ring. The National Anthems were played. It was touching that after a few seconds the fidgeting, grinning, gum-chewing lines of boys, and scatter of girls, swelled in the pride of the music. For Wales, a recording of a male voice choir boomed out a sonorous and oaky anthem; a hundred mellow voices from the hills. It was a contrast to the gruff-voiced, grizzled Irish trainer who grabbed my shoulder before I left the hall. He was shorter than me, and his tracksuit seemed a size too big, but something told me he was shrinking rather than buying the wrong size.

"You're Welsh are you?" he enquired. I nodded. "Do you know Dai Shepherd by any chance?"

"Of course," I said, thinking how it was like asking the magician's apprentice if he'd heard of a guy called Merlin.

"Tell him, if you see him... tell him that Paddy Cochran was asking after him. He'll remember me. Tell him I'll never forget how he saved that lad. Tell him he'll always have a welcome here, he'll want for nothing."

The old man was excited and squeezed affection through his handshake; pressing into my hand his admiration for Dai and his desire for his message be passed on.

"Saved what lad?"

"You don't know about it? Must be maybe twenty years ago now. Dai was over to watch a support bill on a big fight, world title show. He checked into his hotel at the same time as this family; don't know what they were doing in Dublin but there it is. The parents left the wee kiddy playing by the pool.

"We all met at the hotel and none of us noticed; none of us but Dai. That guy's got a sixth sense because the first thing we knew he'd dived in the pool and pulled out the kid. I thought the boy was dead. We all did. Dai worked on him, mouth to mouth, for almost an hour and they were saying 'Give it up, he's gone.' You can't imagine. It was the worst feckin' thing... it wasn't like you see on the TV. It was a mess... a real feckin' mess and the parents... dear God in heaven... but he did it. He brought the kid back, because Dai wouldn't let go of him. He wouldn't give him up and he fought for him I'm telling you; there was no way he was going to give that wee boy up. He was only four."

"And he lived?" I asked, amazed.

"Oh yes, he lived. There was some brain damage, twenty per cent or so, because he was starved of oxygen for so long. We all followed his recovery. And now you'll want to know the amazing part."

He leant towards me and coughed.

I realised how wide my eyes were.

"They say he did it twice. They say he's saved two people from feckin' drowning. So you tell him I'll never forget him saving that kiddy. Tell him Paddy Cochran was asking after him. He'll tell you all about it."

Though it was the first time I'd ever heard the story, I always knew. It was Dai and his invisible net.

The Welsh squad screamed themselves hoarse for both Madoc and Josie. I yelled Josie on, as the stockier

Scottish girl tried to pick her punches. Josie backed the girl up time and again; cutting her off, cutting down the ring angles. Having trapped her opponent, Josie launched a two-fisted attack. The bell went for the end of the second round.

I didn't see exactly what had happened, but before she came out for the third, something went on between her and Colin. He raised his voice and I caught something about her having to cool down. The ref asked if everything was alright. They nodded.

By the third round, the Scot was desperately fighting for it, but Josie never lost her control – stabbing out a jab as sharp as a sewing machine needle. Her opponent was dazed by a good number of lefts to the face in quick succession. When the unanimous decision was announced, Josie was rightly assured of silver or gold and was through to box at the same time as me, 3pm on Saturday. But after the fight Colin and Josie stalked off in opposite directions.

Madoc also got through to the finals in spectacular style. His opponent hardly landed a shot.

Josie and I watched TV for a while after we'd eaten. Our hotel was in the St Stephen's Green area. Down in the street below, a drunken group of women were dancing; it looked like a hen party. Josie was restless, dangling a kicking foot off the bed.

"Let's get out of here. I'm bored. It's bloody Friday night."

"Won't they mind?" I asked. The rules on squad were that we had to be in bed by 10.30pm and I assumed the same, or possibly more, restrictions applied here.

"I'm not talking about getting pissed. My boyfriend said we've got to visit this famous pub, Gogertys. I even heard Colin talking about it on the coach. Let's find it. We can always have a diet coke or an orange juice... pick you up a nice Irish feller."

"Yeah, right, like that's going to happen." I thought it over. "Let's just go for one then but don't let me do any dancing."

We headed, under Josie's direction, to Grafton Street.

It was the worst start to an evening. Dublin was awash with a torrential downpour, which had everyone racing for cover. The rain channelled down my neck and back. Solemn heads were bowed under hoods and brollies, giving the masses hurrying beside the towering churches a weather-enhanced reverence. I followed after Josie and, even in the rainstorm, I marvelled at the Georgian architecture and the streetlamps, delicate as copperplate.

"Are we there yet?" I shouted above the rain. We had turned left off Grafton Street and Josie was walking even faster.

"Just up there, Dame Street!" A second later we darted through the door of Gogertys.

"This is ok," Josie said, as her reedy figure was bumped by standing drinkers.

"I love it... I love the music," I said, tapping my foot. "I like the chairs too," I said, more to myself than Josie.

"Huh?"

"They've got harps carved into the backs."

"You're such a tourist," she snapped. "You think Irish people really sit on chairs like that?"

"I'm not stupid, and I am actually a tourist. The Welsh Tourist Board should look into chairs with daffs in the back."

"Whatever."

"You Welsh?" the barman asked with thick brogue.

"Sure am," I said, as Josie and I joined the queue.

"How do you like Dublin?" he asked.

"Fabulous," I yelled, over a group of enthusing American tourists shaking themselves out of their rucksacks. To annoy Josie I followed it up with "Great chairs!"

"Why don't you bugger off and get us a couple of those bloody chairs you're so keen on, huh?" she said.

I grabbed a table and noticed the rain had eased, leaving a film of moisture suspended in the air; saving the space for more rain to come. The damp surroundings were as right as the tourist trappings; as fitting as the Irish reel coming from the three players. The old tunes fell from wooden walls like tapestries. Of course it was touristy, but you couldn't help but love it. Gogertys was as cosy as sitting round a farmhouse fireplace with autumn weather kneading the kitchen door.

The musicians slipped out to the street, taking advantage of the break in the rain and huddling on the corner to smoke. A waiter weaved his way past with an order of spring cabbage, colcannon and a slab of pink bacon. An early Avril Lavigne song came on as Josie placed a half pint of Guinness on the mat in front of me.

"Hey, I can't have that," I said. "We're fighting. Plus, I don't know if I'll like it."

"You can't come to Dublin and not have Guinness. It's good for you. Don't be so wet and keep an eye out for Pickle. I don't want him showing up."

"You really don't get on with him do you?" I said, surveying the bar and the door.

"His attitude is all wrong," Josie said. "Great for the boys, just great... but girls? He's got to have more faith in us, put more faith in us. How're we supposed to get anywhere with him putting us down. You've seen what he's like with that Zoe from Cwmgors, always on about how big she is."

"I know what you mean but I don't think it's a deliberate thing. I'm pretty sure if he thought about it he wouldn't be so obvious." The Guinness settled in my stomach like soup.

"Even if he was more subtle, how's that any improvement? Look, I'm not being funny but I've got more experience than you. Do you know what I mean? I've been away before with Colin; I've talked to the other girls on the international circuit. I know how it works."

"Sure, but it takes time I suppose. All this is new, only from last September. I'm just saying that before last September we had nothing and now look at us, we're in a pub in Ireland and we're boxing tomorrow!"

"I don't reckon you'd be so grateful if you knew what was going on behind the scenes. Haven't you noticed that Colin has been trying to get Alana up to 63kg? That's your weight and Emma's weight and Kathy's been starving herself to go down to that weight? Listen, they can take maybe one or two girls only each tour. Know what I mean? It goes without saying that there are more matches for girls around 63kg. But this is the thing... to get sponsorship and funding Colin has to get the girls to win medals otherwise forget it, squad goes nowhere. So he's got his key four, yeah? There's me, and I'm not being big-headed, and there's Alana, Hayley and Vicky. What he's going to have to do for a couple of years is slide the four of us up and down the weights and if we have some success maybe at some point we'll get some more money and then more get to go away. Fair enough, but he's not that bothered in the first place.

"The rest of the squad, including you, end up training their asses off for nothing. You wouldn't be here yourself if Alana hadn't bruised her shoulder sparring and you know it too. You think you did ok in Norway but Colin told Phil he couldn't take a chance and send you again. If you can't guarantee a medal you're wasting your time, but how can you get a medal if you can't get experience?"

"Shit."

It put a different spin on things. It seemed to me that the leading cast had been picked and it wasn't like there was even a chorus. The rest of us would be competing to understudy, fighting and doing hundreds of press-ups, sit-ups, running and weighing ourselves over and over again. I understood. Alana had picked up a minor injury and had been forced to rest up for a bit. I'd been lucky that Cleto had been in the gym to hold the pads or I would have been unprepared. The guys were getting old, and Tony was struggling to hold pads even strapped into his weightlifting belt. I'd thought it was unfortunate that Alana wasn't around for sparring. I hadn't realised I wouldn't have gone to Ireland if she had been.

"Yeah," continued Josie, "but imagine what we could all do, all of us, if we had the encouragement. You should see the confidence in the other squad teams and that's how they win. It's the confidence. It's the mental attitude and they've also got the funding, the sponsorship, even England..."

"Don't you bloody know it all!"

Josie and I froze. I wondered how much he'd heard but it didn't matter anymore, I knew I was finished. I leant forward and hid my drink behind my elbow, chin in hand. Colin's eyes took on the swarthy blackness of his Guinness as he took a pull on the pint and his sneer pushed up the pearl foam. I noticed the tattoos on his knuckles; scratched smudges of blue script like he'd done it at home.

"Sponsorship?" he growled. "What the hell do you know about sponsorship? Two years ago they gave England four and a half million pounds for amateur boxing. How much do you think they give Wales? Go on... tell me, bloody know all. How much did they give Welsh Amateur Boxing? You know so much."

Josie hadn't looked at him until this point but she seemed suddenly to scaffold her thin skeleton as if to brave it out. She met his eyes, and the air blistered between them.

"No? No idea? Miss I-know-so-much-about-everything-I-think-I'll-take-over-myself? I'll tell you then, they gave Wales just under ninety-seven thousand. He clutched an imaginary purse and puckered lips. So you know what you can do with all your frickin' 'ooh, the English girls have nice tracksuits'. It's only in the last couple of years we've had the money to buy the boys' kit. Before that they had to beg, steal or borrow."

I remembered Alana at the last squad in her old-as-Biggles head guard and the way her thumb stuck through her right glove. It was all Tony had spare.

"If you've finished, I think you'll find I'm entitled to my opinion," Josie returned but her gaze had shifted.

I made as if I was interested in one of the wall posters that I could see over the heads of the drinkers. I stared at a print of some flame-haired folk guy, Luke Kelly, and it said he was in *The Dubliners* 1962 – 1984. He must have been the lead singer because his mouth yawned around a microphone. Gramps had loved *The Dubliners*, along with the Welsh-Irish folk of *The Hennesseys*. With relief I spotted Tony, who eased through the Americans, oblivious to the drama.

"Alright Babes?" Tony smiled and I stayed still, letting only my eyebrows say hello.

"I haven't finished, Josie," Colin continued, ignoring Tony's entrance, "but you bloody have. All that shit in the ring today, the 'don't do that' with the shorts. That's how we cool you down, how we've always cooled boxers down. It's thanks to you that I've been on the phone to Phil Jones saying we'll have to afford a goddamn female liaison officer. This is exactly what I was afraid of, constant bitching and none of you do a frickin' thing you're told. I'm pulling you out Josie. I don't want you on the squad anymore. I won't have attitudes on squad. You're off and you can get the hell out of this pub while you're at it! Bloody women."

"You're a prick," Josie said.

"Wear this," spat Colin, and he threw his full pint at her. The barman yelled something.

Josie jumped clear of the black arc and went for Colin. I held her back by her shoulders.

"Come on," I said. "Let's get out of here."

We slunk out, and in the cool air Josie swore to herself.

"Bloody hell," I said.

"Screw him, I'll box for England. Pickle is an effin' prick, a complete effin' prick."

We headed back to St Stephen's as Josie yelled the situation to her boyfriend over her mobile. I walked a polite distance behind and paid even more attention to the architecture.

The next morning Colin scratched through her name on the list. Josie responded by gathering her gear together and leaving. I had no way of stopping her, and I was unsure as to whether I shouldn't go as well. I assumed she caught a bus to the airport and paid for her return flight. Colin said little to me as he was still boiling over.

"A bit of talent and she thinks she's Muhammad Ali. The stupid bloody tart," he grunted.

"Where did she go?" I asked him.

"Probably burning her chest protector... bloody lesbians... and I assume you're staying?"

"Yeah," I said, wishing I'd let Josie knock him out.

Finally, I sat in the red vest, waiting to watch Madoc box in the finals. I had it on. There was less than an hour to wait before I got to earn it properly, and I still couldn't help being upset about the situation with the girls. I focussed on Madoc as both he and his English opponent ducked through the ropes. They bounced on tip toe, facing each other with a mixture of concentration and curiosity. The round started and they jabbed and parried, circling. The English boy threw out a brisk jab-cross, which Madoc slipped under and darted clear. England-boy composed himself after the miss and launched in again. Madoc merely leaned back clear, rocked forward and hit him sharply with three long left jabs. It continued that way. England was stung.

Madoc stung me too. I wanted to quit right there and I'm not a quitter. What chance did I have at this game? Josie was much more accomplished than me and she was probably clutching her hand luggage somewhere overhead on Ryanair. Madoc, hedgehog-haired teenager, was casually dancing his way to a graceful gold. That's how it should be, I thought.

Madoc started to unload his hooks after getting inside

the other boy's left lead. His opponent grabbed hold and Madoc responded; smashing more punches home. The referee stepped them apart after more clutching. England-boy missed two, landed one, and then, before the bell, Madoc sank in another flurry of crisp shots to the head.

The third round went the same way. When the final bell rang, the Welsh squad got to its feet in anticipation of the result. Both boxers studied the floor as we all waited for the announcement.

Unanimous decision – the red corner – Wales – Madoc Thomas.

We roared.

Fifty minutes later and I was facing my Irish opponent in my red vest. I had never been so nervous. I told myself to keep breathing, because I'd catch myself time and again with my shoulders hunched, holding my breath. I desperately wanted a sip of water. There was no air. I shook my arms out to loosen up. I reminded myself of Madoc's performance.

Be light, graceful, dance, earn the vest.

Perhaps she heard me. At first her shots were nagging point-scorers. Mine were slower but harder as I aimed for her ribcage to slow down her raking left hand. I caught her clean a couple of times, she backed against the ropes and clung to me. As I heaved her away, she grabbed again, and for a moment we were a wrestling knot of determination. I wrenched away and drew back, thinking it was getting scrappy.

She changed tack, dancing back and forth, whisking up a neat lead by counter-punching. I reverted to walking on to her with my defences collapsing around me. I felt a prickle of anger as she show-boated with a classic boxing shuffle. I hit harder and, after feinting a left, my right cross landed with whumping severity. I watched, hopeful that she would fall. She wobbled but recovered quickly. Not hard enough; not by half. I began unconsciously to wind up the punches, desperate. A hook screamed past her, locomotive de-railed, *of course* she had seen it. The hook had been rattling up the track behind me from half a mile away. She rolled back, danced forward and drove home a flurry of corrective jabs.

I clawed back a few points in the third round when she began to grow tired, grappling again, twisting tight enough to wring out my sweat-soaked red vest. *Get off me*, I thought, lurching back. I flashed out a left and then a moment of pure chemistry took me over. A big punch is beyond thought. It happens automatically and it's almost impossible to explain. The actual distance my glove travelled was probably only five or six inches, but the timing of my short, sharp right, was perfect. I felt the force of it reverberate back through me – the kind of punch that should be kept for attackers on dark landings.

I winded her. She pitched forward and crumpled, gasping for air. For a few seconds I was so surprised that I hadn't noticed the referee waving me to the neutral corner. I walked to the corner, gazing at her as she tried to get her breath back. The referee held up his hands in count, then shook his head.

"Over," he mouthed.

A tsunami of sound hit me then from the squad and I tuck-jumped the air in my shorts and vest.

I received my gold medal and they took photographs as the guy behind me holding the flag swept it back and forwards over my head. They played the Welsh national anthem. The crowd cheered and I slapped applause for all of us like a show seal.

"Lucky punch," I heard someone say.

"Yeah, the Irish girl definitely had the cleaner punches, she was unlucky," another replied.

Tony put his arm around my shoulders.

"That's boxing. You were great," he said as he caught hold of the medal and rubbed his thumb across it. "Now's the time to call it a day, Babes. Quit while you're ahead. Still train in the gym but call time on all this."

"Yeah, I know, Tone... I know."

I didn't mind. Things had worked out for me. I had the red vest and a medal and I was going to get my photograph. No one in the world could take it away from me, not even Colin Pickle. I had won, just for a moment.

"I didn't see that one coming," a voice said.

I turned round and messed up the Irish girl's attempt to pat me on the back.

"I haven't seen you before on the circuit have I?" she said, combing through her tangle of damp, blonde hair with her fingers. It prompted me to think about how awful my hair must have looked in the photos. I wanted to put my hands up and smooth it down. I plucked at my bandages instead.

"No, well, except for Norway. Were you there?"

"No, I missed that one but the other girls did well."

"So, do you all box on club shows in Ireland?"

"Are you kidding me? We're not club fighters. I've been on the international circuit since I was sixteen. Our squad only does international and we're all of us medallists – all the established squad girls are. I heard they don't pay you either."

"Pay us, are you kidding?"

"I would've got over 4,500 euros if I'd won, they put it down to expenses but... you know. You can't do this kind of thing and hold down nine to five."

"Yeah."

I figured Josie had heard all this as long ago as Finland. Once I would have risen again to the challenges that squad presented, but I was tired.

It was over.

CHAPTER TWENTY-TWO

When we returned from Ireland, there was a camera crew in the gym, pulled in by Don Rankin and Marshall. The marketing department had me in *The Lawyer* or *The Law Gazette* or something, but wanted me in the *Western Mail* and on TV too. Michael didn't want to get involved so they got a pretend boss from another department to tell the reporter what a dream I was to work with, how dedicated I was, and how much they all supported my extra-curricular activities and such. I didn't mind playing along, although I did half-drown in a ridiculous corporate XXL t-shirt. It seemed all the S/M had been used in Race for Life. The one thing that grated was that they all kept going on about when I was going to turn professional. A girl turning pro in Wales would be no mean feat, but the reporters and the girls in my office went on and on about it as if it was the easiest thing in the world.

Cleto commandeered the news crew and told them how long he'd been training me. I'm not sure he mentioned any sort of gap, but it didn't matter. I smiled and nodded and winked at Tony. Cleto did tell them a nice story about how I'd changed his mind on ladies' boxing and I was touched.

Tony and the guys were overjoyed that their gym had two golds and Harry laughed as Madoc became weary of having to put his arm around me for photographs as we clinked our medals together.

"You make a lovely couple," Harry teased. Madoc stalked off and slumped in a huff next to Ernie.

Once the crew had gone I gathered up all the cups they'd used and began to rinse them out. I snapped the kettle back on as Alana patted me on the back.

"Well done," she said as she drifted past.

The new boxer, Alex, wandered over and tapped at the floor-to-ceiling ball, but he was really only watching the sparring. Looking at him I thought he had nice eyes and a second later, when I realised what a sneaky section of my brain had been thinking, I turned back and busied myself with drying the cups. I still saw them though, big blue eyes, blue as my first red vest. He had a small semi-circular scar above his left brow and I wondered whether boxing was the cause. His hair was alright too. It was coarse, dark blond, thick enough to look kind of dusty. I'd never gone out with anyone who was blond before.

Shut the hell up, I instructed myself. *As if.*

Tony called time and the sparring ended.

"You can't half punch," Alex said to me, as the boxers in the ring sucked at the bottles held out to them, like newborn calves leaning over a fence. "I saw you the other day on the pads with Cleto. I'd hate to be your boyfriend."

"It's worse than that. I'm also crap at cooking," I retorted, still hooked on the word boyfriend. *Boyfriend.*

"Do you have anything going for you at all?" he asked, his face lighting up with a smile.

"Sure, I'm good with words and I can type fast. Which could be useful if you're illiterate."

"That's a shame. I've been able to write my own name for a while now. Alex Armstrong." He stuck out his bandaged hand and I shook it.

"Good boxing name! I'm Lizzie," I said. I was already confused. I couldn't tell if he was merely being friendly. I didn't know whether Fay and Harry had convinced me there was something there when there wasn't. I told myself to get perspective. He was being friendly, nothing more. But I was left unable to concentrate.

A hard training session put me right and for a time I forgot he was there, forgot the world was there.

Before I left, he came over.

"Since you're a crap cook I might have to ask you out for a meal at some point."

"Oh, um... ok." I couldn't believe I'd told him I was good with words.

"Great," he replied. "I'll leave you get changed... but I'll hold you to that."

I closed the door of the changing rooms and sat on the shell chair with my head in my hands, sighing in the smell of mildew. I asked myself what the hell I had gone and done.

CHAPTER TWENTY-THREE

I went up to the gym again; winding through the dun-coloured houses that had come at the slope sideways. It's there that the shed sits, on the outskirts of the council development, before the roads stretch out over the mountain to where the horses run.

Down at the end of Lonely Street...

I did my training as usual and afterwards braved the streaky dirt of the shower walls and the uneven sprinkler, which dribbled out a watery Morse code. My hands trembled as I applied my eyeliner, peering over the rose-pink chair to see in the mirror.

I opened the door to be confronted by Tony, who was wearing a white t-shirt on his head.

"Very bridal, Tone," I said, as I pulled it off him and threw it onto a chair. "He'll be here soon," I warned.

"Aye," said Harry. "I'm going to give you away and Tony and Ernie want to be bridesmaids."

"I haven't even been out with him yet, and that's if he turns up at all!"

"We want to hear all about it too. Everything! He best not mess you around."

"You're making me more nervous. I'm going to wait outside."

"Aw, Lizzie... "

"Let her go," said Dai Shepherd with a smile.

These guys had taken my affection and returned it like a counter punch.

Waves of mountain wind batted at my hair and reddened my ears. I stood against the breeze, resolute. I closed my eyes. Below the draughts of air I could hear my heartbeat, my own rhythm, and I could hear a car pulling across the gravel. I opened my eyes.

Seconds out.

Time.

ABOUT THE AUTHOR

Louise Walsh is thirty-four years old and lives in Cardiff where she also works as a legal secretary. She has always loved writing and boxing and is a member of Cardiff Writers' Circle. *Fighting Pretty* is her first novel.

ACKNOWLEDGEMENTS

There are many people who helped inordinately with this book. Firstly, a huge thanks to my editor, Penny Thomas, and to Jen Campbell, together with everyone else at Seren. Thanks also to Cardiff Writers' Circle, whose constructive criticism and support has been invaluable. Thanks to Brenda Gibbins and Hugh Lester who helped me find my voice many years ago, although it took me a while to use it.

I would like to thank my friend Zoe Gauci, for her understanding. May all your dreams come true, Flo. I'm also grateful to my old friend Dave Carter, for being there the first time I ever threw a punch, and countless since.

In addition thank you to John Graham and Nick Owen for their generous sponsorship, and also the rest of the staff at William Graham Law Ltd for their kind support. And also thanks to everyone at Dave's Gym.

Thanks also to Phil Tunnicliffe and his group, *The Cheatin' Hearts*, Josh & Lawrence Haggerty, Lana Cooper (who in May 2008 became the first female boxer in Wales to turn professional) & Bobbie Cooper,

Amanda Carpenter, Leo Abse Cohen Solicitors, Mick Tinning, John Roberts, Kay Smith and Pat Brooks, Jonathan Green, John Ledsam and Steve Robinson.

Lastly, I have to thank everyone at the Gelligaer boxing gym who were the inspiration. Without meeting them, this novel would never have been written.